STILLWATER
SMITH

By Frank Roderus

STILLWATER SMITH

FRANK RODERUS

DOUBLEDAY & COMPANY, INC.
GARDEN CITY, NEW YORK
1986

Library of Congress Cataloging-in-Publication Data
Roderus, Frank.
    Stillwater Smith.
    I. Title.
PS3568.O346S7   1986   813'.54   85-20420
ISBN 0-385-23066-4
Copyright © 1986 by Frank Roderus

For John and Kay Theobald

STILLWATER
SMITH

CHAPTER 1

The warm, pungent odors of the store surrounded him as he stepped through the door and by habit removed his hat. He paused there for a moment, relishing the scents that reached him. The sharp tang of the smoked meats, hams and bacon and strings of cased sausages suspended from the beams to his right. Whale oil and machine oil and cod liver oil. Pickling brine. Salt. Burlap. And underlying it all the scent of tobacco, the fresh scents of stored twists and the ancient ones of tobacco long ago burnt and savored and exhaled into the air within the log walls of the old store.

The right corner of Smith's mouth curled slightly in a hint of smile. Old store, indeed. He had been in the valley longer than the store had been here. He could remember the dull thunk and thump of the axes when the logs were cut to raise these walls. By that man and his sons. What had their names been? He could not remember now. Or did not bother to, anyway. They were long gone. Moved on to more exciting prospects. Ben Frake had been in the place eight, nine years now. And before him there had been Jonas Smith. No relation. No one named Smith had relations in this country.

Smith thought about that, acknowledging it as a simple fact without overtones of regret, and shuffled toward the counter where Frake was already waiting on two men Smith had never seen before. Smith's gait was slow and patient, and his right foot dragged across the scuffed and worn puncheon flooring. Normally he moved with a slow, fluid ease, but the sole of his right shoe was coming loose. He needed thread to repair it. It was the reason he had come down this week.

"Be with you in a minute, Smith," Frake said and went back to showing his customers an assortment of pins and brooches on a velvet-lined display board.

Smith nodded and turned away to finger through a pile of clothing on the nearest shelf. A new shirt caught his eye, sturdy wool and forest green, but that could wait. Sometime before fall he would have to buy a new union suit, though. A man had no choice about that.

He glanced idly back toward the counter. He was in no particular hurry, merely avoiding temptation.

The customers were cowboys. That was obvious. They were booted and spurred, and faintly shiny wear lines showed on their trousers where chaps would normally be belted although there was no need for such protective riding gear up here. They had gauntleted gloves tucked behind their belts and did not give a thought, or seem to, to wearing their wide-brimmed hats indoors. That was a convention Smith had never been able to accept. He had been taught early that a man does not wear his hat indoors.

Cowboys, Smith thought, so there was livestock in the valley again. Stockmen had come occasionally before and others before them. The prospectors first, but they went away disappointed. Meat hunters. Loggers. Gandy dancers and tie cutters when the railroad was being built down below. Sheepherders. Trophy hunters. A good many had come through. Not so many had stayed. Smith had seen them all. He could not have said that he came to know any of them particularly well.

"That one's pretty," one of the cowboys was saying.

What they saw was not imposing. He was a lean, gray man with flesh and clothing alike worn by time and weather.

His hair had once been dark. Now it was mostly gray. The heavy stubble of beard on his cheeks was nearly white and almost thick enough to hide the deep wrinkles that creased his face and neck. He shaved once a week, every Sunday morning, and this was Saturday afternoon. His hair was nearly as ragged as his clothing. Once each month, more or less, he cut it himself with shears that a more particular workman would have discarded.

All of the original buttons on his shirt had been replaced with wood disks cut from cross sections of twigs, and the hat that he held in a leathery hand was shapeless and battered. The hat might once have been a snappy kossuth in issue black, but the felt had long since lost any semblance of rigidity and the years had given it the color of earth and dust.

The man himself was thin, with long, ropy muscles and a pronounced stoop to his narrow shoulders. His eyebrows were bushy and dark over a long, narrow nose and wide, thin-lipped mouth.

His eyes, though, were clear, bright and steady. And of such an extremely pale blue or gray that it was impossible to determine which their color was.

At the moment the pupils glittered like shards of obsidian from his anger.

"What the hell is this to you, mister?" Tuck demanded. His friend Bill, even though Bill was the one who seemed to have plans for the evening, was silent.

Smith's expression did not change as he struggled with the anger that was souring his stomach. He willed himself to remain calm and deliberately forced the tension from his body.

"How much?" the other asked.

"A dollar seventy-five," Ben Frake answ

The one who had asked the question sh
"Too much for what I got in mind."

The other cowboy winked at him and dug ar
his ribs. "Ask the man what he's got for a qua.

Bill snickered and punched his buddy on the ;

Frake reached over the more attractive cameos ;
glass costume jewelry to pick up a gaudy little baub
show it to them. "This is only forty-five cents. Ge.
silver and paste. The quality"—he shrugged—"it isn't
for the price."

Bill took the pin from him and held it to the ligh
"What do you think, Tuck?"

His friend grinned. "Ought to be good enough if what
we've heard is true, Bill."

"I'll take it." Bill dropped the pin into his shirt pocket
and dug into his jeans for a coin. He paid Frake and accepted his change.

"Anything else, boys?" Frake asked.

"Not for me," Bill said. "I got places to go and things to
do."

The other cowboy, Tuck, laughed and rolled his eyes.
He winked at his buddy again and began to loudly whistle
"Oh! Susanna." "Right, Bill?"

Bill snickered.

Smith felt a swift and most unexpected surge of anger
that churned in his stomach and brought the taste of bile
to the back of his throat.

"Hold it," he snapped. He spoke before he thought. In-
stinctively. There was a sharp, controlled ring of command
in his voice.

The two cowboys stopped where they were and stared at
him.

"The girl," he said in a voice of soft reason. "You're new here, but you've heard things. Maybe someone forgot to tell you that she isn't right. She isn't right mentally."

He was speaking to Bill, the one who had bought the gewgaw, but Bill refused to meet his eyes. They had been told. It was Tuck who answered.

"She's grown, isn't she?" he said.

"No," Smith said softly. "She never will be." The anger was fading now, being replaced with reason and patience. He was glad. He smiled at the cowboys. The expression was genuine. He did not have to fake it. "It's a matter of taking advantage, boys. I don't think you would want to do that. It isn't even necessary. There's a woman who lives downvalley. Her name is Nelly, and she is very pleasant company." He smiled again. "And inexpensive. I can show you where she lives."

Bill gave his friend a troubled look. He seemed to be embarrassed at having his intentions caught out. As he should be, Smith thought without rancor. It was only Tuck who was showing any belligerence about it.

"Smith is right, you know," Ben Frake put in. "Susanna is a child. Folks around here feel protective toward her. You should know that."

Bill glanced down toward the shirt pocket where he had put the bauble. He shrugged. He had given up the game. There was anger twisting Tuck's face, though. He bunched his hands into fists and took a step toward Smith. Bill stopped him with a tug on his shirt sleeve.

"Did the man say your name was Smith, sir?" Bill asked.

"That's right."

"We'll be thanking you for the advice, Mr. Smith, and apologize for not knowing the way things were," Bill said.

Tuck clouded up again and would have said something,

but Bill stopped him with a jerk on his sleeve. Bill leaned close to his friend and whispered something.

Whatever was said, Tuck did not like it. He looked from Smith to Bill and back to Smith again. But after a moment he gave in. He nodded and said something, and Bill released his grip on Tuck. The two of them nodded to Ben Frake and left the small store, their spurs chiming lightly with every impact of bootheel against wood.

Smith felt the last remnants of tension leave him. He had not even known he was holding himself so tightly until he felt himself relax. He sighed.

He fished into his pocket for the scrap of paper where he had written down his requirements. A spool of waxed cotton harness thread to fix his shoes. A twist of tobacco. Bag of salt. Keg of cornmeal, cheaper than flour and just as nutritious. Saleratus. Coffee beans.

Fishhooks. He had forgotten to put those on the list, but he was running low again. He would have to tell Frake to add them to the list.

He looked at the storekeeper and was surprised to see amusement in the man's eyes. Smith found nothing in that encounter that he would consider remotely funny.

"What is it?" he asked reluctantly.

Frake's belly jiggled, and he began to laugh. "You. Those boys. They heard the name, by Godfrey, and acted like you were some kind of gunsel, the way they turned around and got out of here." He chuckled. "That's all."

"Oh," Smith said dully.

It was, he supposed though, cause for amusement at that. It was no secret in the valley that the local recluse never shot anything, not even for meat. When the deer or elk became so bothersome that he had to chase them away from his garden he bought leftover Fourth of July fireworks to scare them with.

Probably that was something of a joke too, he thought as he handed Frake his list.

The storekeeper filled the order quickly, and Smith paid and left without further conversation. He sighed with exasperation as he climbed back into his wagon and spoke gently to his team to get their attention before he took up contact with their bits.

He had forgotten to tell Frake about the damned fishhooks.

But he did not feel like going back inside again. They would just have to wait until next time.

He wheeled Jake and Jack into a smart turn and headed back up the valley at a long trot, enjoying watching the smooth bunching and thrusting of their powerful haunches as they moved.

CHAPTER 2

He came awake abruptly, bolt upright on the narrow bed
and eyes wide, with no recall whatsoever of any period
between deep sleep and complete wakefulness. And with
no conscious awareness of what it was that had wakened
him.

No conscious knowledge, but he knew, in spite of that.

With a shudder, a quick shaking of his shoulders to
throw off the chill that raced briefly up his spine, Smith
shoved the blanket aside and swung his legs around so that
he was sitting on the edge of the bed. He ran a hand over
his chin—it was Sunday morning, time to shave again—
and on across his scalp.

There was no point in trying to go back to sleep again.
He would not be able to. He knew that from long experience. The quick, never remembered night frights happened
from time to time. Not so often now as they used to, but
more often than comfort would have decreed. Now that he
was awake he was up for the day, like it or not.

He glanced toward the window he had built into the
front wall of the place. The shutters were open to the night
air, and at this time of year there was no covering over the
empty hole in the wall. During the winter he tacked oiled
paper over it to keep the worst of the winds out. Each
spring he took the paper down. It was possible to buy glass
in the valley now, but it seemed hardly worth the trouble
and the expense. He was used to things this way.

There was nothing to see through the window but darkness. He had no idea how long it would be to dawn, but it felt like it would be a matter of some hours. Certainly it was much too early to begin his choring.

Smith stood and stretched, yawning, not bothering to wish he could get back to sleep. He pulled on his shirt and trousers and stepped into his shoes. He paused for a moment to lift the right foot and turn his ankle so that he could admire for a moment the fact that the shoe sole no longer flapped. The repairs he had made with punch and thread were not pretty, but they worked.

He poured water from a tin bucket into a basin, rinsed his mouth first and then splashed the cold water over his face quickly and was ready for a day that was not yet ready for him. It was too early for breakfast. His stomach would not have tolerated food. A brief, questioning thought of it made him slightly queasy.

Moving by feel and long habit inside the darkened cabin he went to a corner and selected a rod, picked up his creel and tackle box. He also pulled on a jacket. At this altitude there was a sharp nip in the air any time the sun was not shining regardless of the season. With his gear in hand he left the house and found the path leading up to the pond.

He transferred the fishing gear to his right hand and reached down and back with the left, smiling as he did so. The broad head and cold nose were there. He felt the warm, wet lap of a tongue across his palm. Joe had ghosted into his accustomed position without Smith ever hearing the dog move from his bed inside the barn. He scratched the mongrel briefly behind the ears while he walked, then straightened and walked faster so that the exercise would help warm him. He was cold and shivered a little.

Smith followed the path upslope, having no need to see

it in order for his feet to follow it, beyond the low dam to his favorite spot on the south bank.

The original dam had been built by beavers. Over the years, a bit at a time, Smith had dug and hauled barrowfuls of earth and rock to reinforce the beaver-cut saplings until now there was no visible sign of the old structure. But he did not have to see it to know it was there. The pond and the spring that fed it had been his reason for choosing this spot back when he could have located anywhere in the long, gentle valley. He was still happy with his choice.

Smith sat on the rock—his rock—and set the tackle aside. He pulled out his pipe and shaved tobacco into it, tamped and lighted it slowly. He was in no hurry. The dog laid its head on his left thigh for a moment to ask for and receive another ear-scratching, then left him to curl up at his side. Smith puffed on his pipe and allowed a sense of contentment to warm him.

Despite whatever forgotten nightmare had wakened him, he did feel contented now.

The soft glow from his pipe and the even softer shine of the stars overhead were the only lights he could see. There might have been lamps burning in the town but if so they were far below and behind him.

The only sounds he could hear were the low sizzle of burning tobacco whenever he drew on the pipe and the muted chuckle of the water spilling over the dam.

He cupped his hands around the bowl of the pipe, warming them, and solemnly nodded to himself.

This was good. Better, it was the kind of good that could be appreciated even at the moment. That was the best kind of all.

A pang of guilty conscience touched him. He did not deserve this contentment.

But he pushed the twinge out of mind, shoving it away, and drew deeply on the pipe again.

"Joe."

The dog stood, its tongue lolling from its mouth and tail poised to wag, waiting to understand what Smith wanted.

He patted his thigh and the dog draped its forepaws over his lap. It was too big to actually sit in his lap, had been since it was still a pup, so it lay half across him with its hind legs still on the ground and allowed Smith to fondle its ears and rub the massive head affectionately.

CHAPTER 3

The visitors came just as Smith was finishing his chores. It was well past dawn, and he had already had his breakfast —fresh trout fried in a coating of cornmeal—and had shaved. The horses had been fed, and Smith was completing the Sunday-morning ritual of thoroughly grooming each of them. Every other morning of the week they ate at dawn and received only a cursory brushing. Sundays the heavy, coarse-boned but sleek and willing workhorses were entitled to their day of rest.

When he heard the approach of saddle horses Smith dropped Jack's huge off forefoot—another few weeks and he would have to pull their plates and reset them—and straightened. He bent backward a little to relieve the kink caused by the bending, then walked out into the glare of the midmorning sun to see who was coming.

Having any visitor here was rare. Having someone come to call horseback was nearly unheard of.

The riders were already in the bare gravel yard between the house and barn. There were three of them. A heavyset man in his late fifties or early sixties who wore a dark suit and bow tie as if they were a uniform and had the ramrod carriage and tall seat, in spite of his wealth of stomach, to magnify that impression. A lanky man in vest, sleeve garters and broad hat who carried a rifle in a saddle scabbard. And the cowboy named Tuck who had been in the store the previous afternoon. Smith waited for their approach with no sign of welcome.

The older man took the lead.

He was a big man apart from his belly, with thick, once handsome features and muttonchop side-whiskers that bracketed a pink, freshly shaved complexion and a slightly bulbous nose. He wore a pale, narrow-brimmed hat and boots that were freshly blacked and obviously expensive. The boots alone probably cost the equivalent of a half year's wage for a workingman, and Smith could not even guess at the value of the ring that was sparkling on the little finger of the man's left hand.

Smith folded his arms and waited silently for the man to explain himself. He did not invite them to dismount. They stopped a few feet away from Smith, the big man in the center of their little party and the other two flanking him a pace or two to the rear.

Smith felt neither pleasure at the prospect of an unexpected visit nor any particular apprehension, but he could not help but admire the horse the big man was riding. Tuck and the other man were on ordinary cow ponies of the sort to be found in any remuda, but their boss was riding a tall and exceptionally handsome blood bay. Probably Cleveland Bay breeding, Smith guessed. He openly admired the animal, ignoring the men.

The big man frowned. "Mr. Stillwater Smith?"

Smith nodded, his eyes still running over the points of the bay. Strong forelegs set wide against a deep-chested barrel. Ideal slope to the shoulders. Finely molded head with a broad poll. Eyes calm. Ears forward and alert. He noticed that the muzzle and ears had been shaved, and the coat had been groomed to a high gloss. Smith doubted that the man riding the horse had done that meticulous grooming, though.

"I am Asa Wheeler, Mr. Smith."

Smith continued his inspection of the horse. Good horseflesh was something he truly appreciated, and this animal was as good as he had seen in a great many years.

"May I get down, Mr. Smith? I have business to discuss with you." There was more than a hint of irritation in Wheeler's voice.

Smith's pale eyes left the horse and rose to meet Wheeler's. Deliberately he hesitated for a moment. Then he nodded. "If you wish."

All three men dismounted, and Tuck moved quickly to take the reins from his employer. Nothing changed in Smith's expression, but he felt a moment of quiet amusement. Ask Tuck—or any cowboy—if he had a master, and the response would be loud and indignant. Cowhands considered themselves the freest and most independent of men. But this one had a master whether he knew it or not.

"These gentlemen," Wheeler said, "are Charles Devore, my foreman, and John Friar, top hand and unofficial segundo."

John Friar would, of course, be Tuck. Smith was not familiar with the term segundo but could guess at the probable meaning. Likely a corporal to Devore's sergeancy. Any finer distinctions held no meaning here.

"Come inside, gentlemen." Smith turned and led the way into his home. The log home was tidy and sparsely furnished, almost sterile, even though he had lived in it the better part of fifteen years now. There were the bed, a table with two chairs, an armchair with a reading lamp suspended from the wall above it, a stove and cabinets against the back wall. There were no pictures or calendars hung and no curtains at the window. A wooden footlocker was placed at the foot of the bed. A book with a scrap of cloth placed between the pages for a marker lay on the floor beside the armchair. Smith picked that up and placed it on top of the footlocker.

Wheeler took it in at a glance and must have noticed the scanty provisions for seating. He motioned with his hand, and Devore went back outside. Tuck was still tying their horses.

"Coffee, Mr. Wheeler?" There was still some left from breakfast. He looked at Wheeler for a moment and amended, "Or would you prefer Colonel to Mister?"

"Major," Wheeler corrected. "But Mister will do under the circumstances."

"All right."

"Yes, I would like some coffee. Thank you."

Smith nodded and poured the leftover but still hot beverage into the two cups he owned. He had neither sugar nor canned milk to offer with it so served it black without comment. Wheeler helped himself to one of the two chairs at the small table, and Smith took the other.

"You made a point of bringing up an old title, Mr. Smith. Must you question me now about my loyalties? I hope not. I sincerely hope, sir, that you are not one of those Southern, uh, gentlemen who foster ancient resentments."

"I don't recall saying I was from the South, sir."

Wheeler smiled slightly. "Unnecessary, Mr. Smith. The accent is still there, faint and almost faded but still there." He sighed. "Lest the question arise, then, I once wore Yankee blue and proud of it. But I want you to know that that is long behind us now. Long behind, sir. I came to offer a business proposition, not to rehash old disputes."

Smith nodded and took a sip of his coffee. It would have served no purpose to point out that it was Wheeler and not he who had raised the question of past loyalties.

"What I have in mind, Mr. Smith, is the purchase of water rights from you."

"I have no water to sell, Mr. Wheeler. The stream is not mine. It only crosses my land."

"Actually you may have more right in the matter than you realize. But let me explain. I am the controlling principal in a cattle-raising enterprise, Mr. Smith. My partners and I raise beef on a fairly substantial scale. We intend to use high pasture land, which we recently purchased from the government, for summer finishing of our steers. Do you follow me so far?"

Smith nodded. He was not particularly familiar with livestock raising, but cattle and sheep had been brought up to the high grass from time to time almost since Smith had gotten here.

"We made a most attractive deal on the grazing rights along both sides of this valley. However, we lack water on the land involved. And as you probably know, the lands immediately adjoining the water are held in private ownership. What we propose, Mr. Smith, is to divert a flow of water from your property and channel it to the south. Onto the land we control."

Smith raised an eyebrow. The idea seemed unnecessarily complicated. And probably in violation of a law no man could repeal, the one that decrees that water must surely run downhill.

"I understand your confusion, Mr. Smith, but please let me explain. The water in its present course follows a natural flow starting high on your property and continuing through it to the valley below. However, my engineers report that it would be possible to make a cut in the natural embankment on the south side of the stream, digging at a point approximately a quarter mile above your dam. An excavation seventy-eight yards long to an average depth of fourteen feet would be required. That would present no problem whatsoever. I would propose to build diversion gates at the point where the cut enters the natural stream bed. Water could be channeled through the original course to meet your needs, including the maintenance of your pond." Wheeler smiled. "As you may have gathered by now, Mr. Smith, we have done our homework rather thoroughly. Water surplus to your needs would be directed onto our land quite easily by way of a ditch."

"What about the people downstream?" Smith asked.

"We foresee no problem whatsoever, Mr. Smith. The ditch we propose would be routed onto our land and then back, across the bottom reaches of your property, into the original stream bed again. The supply of water downstream would be only slightly diminished by our uses. I doubt that the volume removed would even be noticeable."

Smith grunted. Wheeler's idea sounded entirely reasonable. And entirely too complicated. Well prepared, though. He wondered when these engineers had made their surveys. And why—and *how*—they had managed to do their work without his knowledge.

"In exchange for the use of your property to create our gates and diversion ditches, Mr. Smith, we would be prepared to pay you a substantial sum," Wheeler went on. "We would, of course, guarantee, in writing, the preservation of flow for your own personal needs. Our attorney has already thoroughly researched the applicable laws as to water rights and utilization, and we have a proposed contract for you to consider. Upon signing of the contract by both parties, Mr. Smith, we are prepared to pay you an initial trespass fee of one thousand dollars in cash monies and an annual fee thereafter of one hundred dollars."

"I assume you have a copy of this proposed contract that I can read?"

"Of course, sir, although I don't have it with me at the moment."

That was odd, Smith thought. He wondered why the man had bothered to come all this distance to speak to him yet neglected to bring a copy of the document for Smith to go over. And he was still wondering about those engineers Wheeler had mentioned.

"Before I'd even consider it," Smith said, "I'd want to go over the gate and ditch sites with you or your people. And I'd have to have a look at the contract too, of course."

"Of course." Wheeler sounded pleased. "At your convenience, Mr. Smith."

A thought occurred to him and he asked, "You already have cattle in the valley, don't you?"

"A few head, yes. Devore and his people brought three hundred head of two-year-olds onto the land this past week."

"Where are those cattle drinking now, Mr. Wheeler?"

"We obtained a temporary trespass lease from a Mr. Malcolm Barber," Wheeler said. "A lane across the lower end of his property so our animals can reach the natural stream bed."

"I see." Smith nodded. "All right, Mr. Wheeler, I'll consider your proposal. I'll make you no promises beyond that, but I will consider it. You say you can have one of your people go over the ground with me at my convenience?"

"That is correct, sir."

"Dawn tomorrow then, Mr. Wheeler. Have him bring a copy of the contract with him, please."

Wheeler looked positively delighted. He stood and offered Smith his hand. "Thank you, Mr. Smith. Thank you very much. I believe it will be a pleasure doing business with you, sir."

Smith shook the man's hand but made no comment beyond that. Nor any promises.

Wheeler, he noticed, had not touched the coffee he had been given.

For some reason that irked Smith. Not a great deal, but there was nevertheless that small sting of resentment. He pushed the feeling aside.

CHAPTER 4

When the shade from the roof of the small barn reached the base of the second corral post, Smith leaned forward, allowing the front legs of his chair to come back to the earth with a thump. He dropped his pipe, cold now, into a pocket and carried the chair back inside the house. It was well past lunchtime, but he had not eaten since breakfast. It was not that he had not had time to eat. He had simply forgotten. Now his stomach rumbled a little, but now he did not have time to prepare himself a meal. There would be time enough for that later.

He put the chair in its proper place at the table and again gathered up his fishing gear, selecting a different rod this time from the one he had used that morning.

The slender rod he chose was seven and a quarter feet long, light and very lively. It had once been longer. Smith found it, discarded by some visiting angler and broken at the base. He had rebuilt it himself, spending several weeks steaming the bamboo lengths apart and shaving them by hand into a lighter, more agile action than the original had possessed, laminating the sections back together with powdered glue he had obtained from Ben Frake and finally refitting the original butt and ferrules. He was pleased with the result.

He carried rod, fly case and creel up to the pond and resumed his place on his favorite rock. A hint of frown pulled at his mouth when he saw that he was alone there.

She was late. He glanced toward the sky, checking the position of the afternoon sun, and decided to give her a little longer before he began to become worried.

He was worried, though. He could not help it. Those men yesterday . . .

Absently he selected a fly from the assortment in his box and tied it onto the horsetail hair he used for a leader. He made his own flies, occupying the evening hours to make them from bits of feather and down and from any stray scraps of fur he might find or pluck.

He glanced across the pond, but there was still no sign of her. He frowned openly. Usually by this time she was here. He hoped nothing had happened to her.

He stood and walked down to the edge of the water, paying out line as he went, leaving a trail of fly, leader and line on the ground behind him. Once he reached the water he stopped and with a practiced flick of the rod tip picked the line up and swung it out over the water. He watched, waiting until the leader had straightened so there would not be too much snap in the return action, then pulled the tip of the rod back to send the lightweight line out behind him.

He continued that way, keeping the line in the air by its own weight with the leader and fly being carried along for the ride. With each forward stretch he laid more line out, until he had the length he wanted in the air. Then he stopped the rhythmic back-and-forward motion, allowing the fly to settle gently to the calm surface of the pond.

The fly floated there, too light to break the surface tension of the water, resting on "legs" that had been made from a tiny puff of rabbit fur he had gathered from a burrow where a cottontail had nested.

Within seconds the fly would begin to waterlog, and then it would sink. Before that could happen he snapped the tip of the rod up, flicking the fly off the water and resuming the back-and-forth pattern with his wrist and forearm, never letting the fly or line touch ground or water. He already was playing all the line he wished to use, but the swift, silent trips through the air were necessary to dry the fur hackles and ensure that the fly would float properly when he again laid it.

Satisfied, he made his cast and let the bit of hooked fluff settle back to the water.

There was movement beyond the pond, and he raised his eyes from the floating fly. As he did so there was a quick, dark surge from under the surface.

Smith looked back, but too late. The trout had already had time to lip the spurious food and to spit it out. He jigged the tip of the rod too late to set the hook at that one brief instant when the fly was inside the fish's mouth. The fish was gone, leaving only ripples behind, and all he succeeded in doing was to destroy the lie of his line.

Across the pond from him, Susanna was laughing. She stood at the edge of the pond with her shoes in one hand and the other placed flat against her stomach as if trying to hold in the glee that was rippling and bouncing there.

"You missed him, Stillwater. You missed that big ol' trout, didn't you?"

Stillwater began to laugh too. "I missed him, Susanna. I surely did."

Her eyes alight with pleasure at the sight of the great fisherman missing such a simple strike, the girl practically bounced through the air as, still laughing, she ran lightly across the dam to his side of the pond.

"You missed him, Stillwater."

"Yes, honey, I did."

She ran to his side and grabbed his right elbow in both her hands, then raised herself on tiptoes so she could give him a wet, happy kiss on the freshly shaven underslope of his jaw. She jostled him when she did it because she was still jumping up and down, literally, with the pleasure of what she had just seen.

"Whoa," he protested. But he was still laughing too. He really did not mind, and the effect of her pleasure was contagious.

He began pulling his line in, hand over hand, hampered considerably by the fact that the girl was still clinging excitedly to his right arm.

CHAPTER 5

Asa Wheeler's man rode into the yard spot on time, just as the morning-red sun was breaking the horizon. Smith was already finished with his chores but had not taken time to eat. He looked at the man Wheeler had sent and decided against a suggestion that they have breakfast together. Smith was choosy about the company he kept.

The man was dressed nearly as well as his employer had been the day before. There was certainly nothing wrong with that, but he held himself in a stiff, unnatural posture of disapproval as he rode into the yard, and there was a pinched, disapproving tightness to the set of his mouth. He gave Smith's home a hooded look that was smug and cold.

Smith decided he did not like Wheeler's employee even before the man dismounted without waiting for permission to do so.

The man introduced himself as Alton P. Taylor. He did not offer his hand.

"Are you the engineer Mr. Wheeler referred to?" Smith asked.

"I am."

Smith nodded and began to walk up the path toward the dam. Taylor hesitated in momentary confusion, then quickly tied his mount to a rail on Smith's corral and hurried to follow.

They walked in silence up the path to the dam, circled around the south side of the pond and continued up a much fainter footpath along the side of the creek for nearly a quarter of a mile to the spring that provided the major flow entering the creek. Beyond that point there was only a trickle of surface runoff feeding the stream, and for most of the year that amounted to no more than a grassy bog.

"All right, Mr. Taylor. I assume you are familiar with the property. Show me what you have in mind."

Taylor was winded from the shallow but steady climb. Probably not used to the altitude, Smith guessed, even though he must have spent some time up here already to have prepared the plans for Wheeler's proposal.

"Down here," Taylor said. He walked back a few rods below the gushing spring outflow and motioned with his hand. "The gate structure will be here, commencing at that spot," he pointed, "and blocking the flow at this angle." Again he pointed. "Standard box construction of milled cypress, which is relatively impervious to damp rot. Gates here and here." He pointed first to a location in the center of the stream and to another on the south bank where they were standing.

"Lift gates, I presume."

"Yes."

"What about the outflow?"

"One gate must be open at all times or—"

"No," Smith interrupted. "I understand that. I meant, where will your ditch be?"

"The canal. Yes." Taylor turned and pointed toward a low-growing juniper some thirty-five or forty yards away. "The center line of the canal will run approximately three and a half feet west of that bush over there, commencing at this point and continuing seventy-eight yards in a direction of one hundred eighty-seven degrees true. At that point it reaches a natural fall line, which of course will have to be enhanced to a depth of approximately three feet and . . ."

Smith was no longer paying attention. He walked to the juniper Taylor had indicated and stood there facing east, looking down across his property to the valley beyond.

It was a lovely sight. He had thought so all those years before when he took up the land, and he thought so still. Even with the encroachment of man-made structures as the town had slowly grown below him in the valley.

From here he could see the early-morning light glinting on his pond. Beyond it was the house, and below that the small creekside field where he raised oats—a short-term crop that was not harmed by cold in its early stages of growth—for his chickens and the work team. On either side of the oat field, which was already coming up high and emerald-green, there was the native grass that was encouraged by the subsurface irrigation from the creek. There, flanking the oats, he cut hay in the late summer to take the horses through the winters.

The quarter section he had taken up, back when he was the only human in the valley and any amount of much better bottom land could have been claimed, was strung out in a long, narrow strip with the creek running through its center. The hundred sixty acres were laid out just under a quarter of a mile wide and slightly more than a mile long.

A hundred sixty acres were regarded as practically nothing in this huge, sprawling country, much of which required very nearly that much land to support a single cow and calf. But to Smith it was everything that he allowed himself to hold dear. And he raised neither cows nor calves. He lived simply, taking in a little cash now and then from the sale of his eggs and the sale of dressed fryers when he butchered the cockerels from his settings of eggs each spring. Apart from that now he occasionally found a little day work to do, mostly involving the hiring of his team more than of himself. None of it brought in very much, but it was enough. More or less.

He sighed. A thousand dollars up front and another hundred a year would make things better. There was no denying that.

But Lord, Wheeler's ditch would be an ugly son of a bitch.

He tried to visualize the change it would make, but his eyes kept insisting on lifting instead to the ring of mountains that surrounded the valley. Jagged peaks surrounded him. Even beyond the mouth of the valley he could see yet another range off in the distance, one massive line of peaks after another, receding into the distance like so many wave tops on a vast ocean that had been frozen into immobility and turned into stone.

Close around the valley the lower mountains were furry with dark green conifers. Above them many extended beyond timberline in great craggy gray-and-white spires. Gray only on the steepest scarps where the snows could not cling. White everywhere else. In the deep, north-facing crevasses where the sun could not reach, the snowfields were very nearly permanent. And for all of the year except during the last and hottest portions of the summers the snow remained on many of the peaks.

Smith sighed again. As different as this country was from everything he had once known, its beauty was awesome. Truly awesome in the old sense of that word. It filled him with awe to look at its grandeur.

He had, quite simply, come to love it.

He probably had not realized that—not to consciously, actively think about it in quite those terms—until now, when he was standing beside an engineer whose intent was to mar a small piece of that beauty by the creation of a raw, artificial ditch.

Smith looked at Taylor and conceded that it was not the engineer's fault. The man wanted to build, not to destroy.

If Smith wanted to become maudlin over the digging of a few feet of ditch, the displacement of a few cubic yards of earth and stone, Taylor would have every right to laugh in his face and point to the horrors done in those valleys where gold and silver ores had been found. Any comparison would have been laughable indeed.

Truly, Smith told himself, he was being silly.

"I suppose you brought a copy of that contract," he said. He was careful that his expression should reveal nothing of what he had been thinking.

Taylor frowned, then snapped his fingers impatiently. "I *knew* I forgot something this morning. Mr. Wheeler gave me the paper last night and told me to not forget to bring it to you, then I came right off and forgot it."

Smith grunted. "Another time, then."

"Did you have any questions about the canal?"

"No." He sighed again. "No, I don't think so." The line Taylor had shown him seemed logical enough from an eyeball appraisal. It would take surveying instruments to prove it out, but it seemed reasonable enough. "No, I don't guess I do."

"Can I tell Mr. Wheeler when you will be down to sign the contract?"

Smith felt tension come into his shoulders, then willed himself to relax. The engineer would have no way to know that no decision had yet been reached. It would be only natural for him to assume that the project would go ahead as planned.

"No," he said. "I'll get word to him."

"All right, I'll tell him that."

They started back down toward the house, Smith slowing his pace so the engineer would not be left behind. The walk back down was considerably easier on Taylor than the climb had been.

CHAPTER 6

Smith puffed absently on the stem of his pipe. A curl of aromatic smoke escaped from the corner of his mouth and hung in the air around his head. He turned a page, tilted the book to a new angle and frowned a little as he had to once again readjust the place where it lay open on his lap. In the past year or so he had become aware that he was having to hold his books at a greater distance. The time would come when he had to buy spectacles or give up his reading. Giving up books would be unthinkable, but there was the question too of expense. He had never bought any spectacles or known anyone who had, not well enough at least to openly ask questions about the process, and he suspected that such a major purchase would be expensive. The thought of Asa Wheeler's trespass payment crossed his mind, and he frowned. Weights and balances. Need against offer. He was far from being sure about how the scale tilted.

His expression moderated and then became a smile as he heard a flurry of activity outside, followed by a low, serious growl. Something, an ermine or a fox perhaps, had come near the coop, but he did not have to worry about it. Whatever the problem, Joe had already taken care of it.

A moment later he heard the soft scrape of the dog's pads on gravel as Joe approached the open door. When Joe wanted to he could move as silently as falling snow, but now that he wanted to be noticed and praised Smith could have heard him coming from fifty yards away.

Smith waited until he saw the dog's muzzle and one eye edge around the doorjamb, then patted his thigh. Tongue out and ears alert, Joe bounded inside the cabin and laid his head in Smith's lap for the reward he had earned. Smith scratched him and rubbed his head for only a moment, then pushed him away. "Back to work now, you old scoundrel, or we'll lose every bird we own."

The dog wagged his tail once and trotted back out into the night.

It had been a long time since Smith had lost any chicks to predators other than the occasional hawk or eagle that Joe could not defend against. Aside from the fact that he could not effectively chase a bird, the airborne predators ranged by day. And Joe had long since appointed himself a night guard. During the daylight hours he frequently roamed away from the place and might be gone for a few hours or the entire day. But he was always back and always on duty before dusk. It was not anything Smith had taught him. It was simply a chore the dog had taken upon himself.

Smith pinched the bridge of his nose, took a moment to relight his pipe and went back to his reading.

CHAPTER 7

Smith scattered the last of the cracked grain on the ground, brushed his hands and carried the empty bucket back inside the coop. The building had been constructed to accommodate chickens, not people. He had to stoop to go through the low doorway and remain bent over inside or bump his head on the dried and creaking saplings he had long ago cut to make the roof.

He rooted through the straw he used for nesting material and began to gather the morning's eggs, transferring them from the nests into the bucket. Most he would pack in sawdust until he had enough to be worth taking in for sale. A few he would save out for his own needs. Eggs fresh from his hens and trout fresh from the pond were his staple diet.

In no hurry, he carried the bucket into the barn and put most of the morning's gather into the crate, slipped the last three in his pocket and set the bucket down beside the barrel where he stored the cracked oats after he had run them through the hand mill.

He moved slowly, comfortably, and took time out to scratch Jack and Jake behind their hairy ears and to rub their muzzles and slip them each an extra handful of the chicken scratch that he filched from the barrel.

This was the fat and easy time of the year. The oat crop had already been planted, and he was months away from the brutal labor of cutting hay and threshing grain. The chicks were old enough to be reasonably sure of survival, and the layers had begun their heavy summer production of eggs. Soon he would have to begin making weekly trips to town just to keep the egg crate from overflowing.

Late spring and early summer were the easy times, when Jack and Jake turned fat and glossy and wild flowers began to dot the bright new grass with yellow and red and blue, when a man could lie in bed until past dawn and not even have to wear a coat when he went out to do his choring. Smith flexed his fingers, spreading his hands wide with the fingers splayed and tightening them into fists again. The winter's aches had left his joints, and he felt good.

He went back into the house and dropped the three eggs into the pot he had already set on the stove to boil. The coffee was ready by then so he poured himself a cup and sat at the table to drink it while he waited for the eggs to cook.

A thin, metallic jangle sounded from the yard, and a moment later he heard the stamp of a horse's hoof and the soft flutter of its nostrils as it blew. Smith looked up in time to see Joe, back already from his morning ranging, cross the doorway with his shoulders hunched and his head held low. The dog's tail was held stiff and straight, and there was no hint of welcome about him although he made no sound. Smith went to the door.

Wheeler's man Tuck was half off his horse, poised there now with one foot still in his stirrup and the other in mid-air.

Tuck looked first at Joe, then, questioningly, toward Smith.

Smith leaned against the doorframe and pulled his pipe out. Tuck took another look at the dog and straightened, throwing his right leg over his cantle and resuming his seat on the horse.

"That dog bite?" Tuck asked.

Smith shrugged and began to shave tobacco into the bowl of his pipe.

The cowhand looked from Smith to the dog and back to Smith again. It was apparent that he was afraid of the dog. The openness of it, the fact that another man could see his fear, made him angry. He scowled at Smith and said, "They told us in town that you're a surly bastard."

Smith tamped the tobacco and lighted it, the stem of the pipe clenched between his teeth. "Surly," he repeated, mouthing the word slowly as if savoring it. After a moment he nodded. "Good word, that. I'm surprised you know it."

Tuck's scowl deepened. He fidgeted in his saddle and shifted his rump as if to step down and give Smith a sound thrashing. But his resolve was broken when he looked again toward Joe. The dog had not moved again. It stood with its head low and hackles up, teeth slightly bared.

"I don't like you, Smith."

Smith nodded again. The bowl of the pipe bubbled and sizzled as he drew on the stem. "Your opinion," he said. "You're entitled."

"I come up here civil and polite to give you a message."

"All right."

"Mr. Wheeler ast me to tell you that he's moved into the Ramey house. He wants to see you there."

"When I come down."

"Tonight," Tuck snapped.

Smith straightened, his lean frame leaving the doorjamb he had been slouched against. Joe took one stiff-legged step forward, and Tuck's eyes cut away from the man toward the dog. "Did Wheeler say to tell me that too?"

Tuck's glance flicked back and forth between the two,

but he was paying more attention to the dog than to Smith. He hesitated for a moment. "No," he said finally.

"When I come down," Smith repeated. His voice was tight now, no longer slow and easy. "Anything more to the message?"

Tuck shook his head.

"Any more messages, you see that somebody else delivers them," Smith warned. He had not liked Tuck to begin with and liked him all the less now. "Now get out of here."

Tuck started to say something, no doubt something full of bluster and bravado, but bit the words back and clamped his jaw shut so hard the muscles ridged and swelled his neck.

Instead he wheeled his horse and raked the animal's sides with the steel rowels of his spurs. The horse jumped forward, more from pain than from obedience, and Smith's mouth twisted in unspoken but useless fury. There was no excuse for treating an animal that way. None.

But there was nothing he could say about it.

Smith stood in the doorway watching until sometime after Tuck had disappeared to the southeast and had more than time enough to clear Smith's land.

He stood like that until the bowl of tobacco was extinguished, then he rapped the pipe against his heel to knock the dottle out and went back inside.

The eggs he had put on to boil were cracked and rubbery, and the pan had boiled nearly dry. Smith grunted to himself and sat down to eat them anyway.

CHAPTER 8

Smith gave Jack and Jake a brief rubdown, checked their feet and led them out to the parked wagon. When the horses were in harness and hitched to the traces he backed the wagon around to the shed and loaded his saws into the bed. He had been toying with the idea of going down and talking to Wheeler, but Tuck had disrupted that. Wheeler could wait.

This was the fat and easy time of year, but that did not mean there was no work to do. Summer was the time to cut the winter's wood, and the earlier the better so the green aspen would have time to dry before it was needed. Smith preferred to burn aspen in his stove. It burned quickly and had to be replenished during the night, unlike heavy chunks of fir, but it burned clean, with little buildup of soot in the chimney. Besides, aspen trees grew almost as quickly as weeds. One man's needs could not begin to diminish a well-established aspen grove. The small suckers that sprang up from the roots beneath the soil were as prolific as they were fast-growing.

He piled his gear into the back of the wagon, a big, broad-toothed felling saw, a smaller bow saw for limbing the downed trees and cutting them into manageable lengths and a pair of wedges and maul in case he needed them too, although the individual aspens were slim and relatively light and easy for one man to drop and handle safely. The bigger firs could be dangerous work even for two men to handle, and Smith had no help.

He climbed onto the driving box, checked to make sure he had his pipe and tobacco and picked up the lines. Jake tossed his head and shook himself like a wet dog when the bit made contact with his mouth, as the big horse always did, and Smith spoke softly to his team. The horses had been working together ever since Smith bought and broke them as a pair of long twos. As one they leaned into the hames and took the load on their shoulders before they started to pull forward with a smooth, gathering flow of power.

Joe appeared from behind the barn, breaking his normal daytime routine of disappearance after the morning's visit, and fell into a trot beside the near front wheel of the wagon.

Smith drove south from the house, taking the team over the small rise beyond which Wheeler intended to run his ditch, and stopped at the top for a moment, more for the view than to let the horses rest from the short climb.

The mountain-rimmed valley lay down to his left. In front of him were the dry-grass slopes that led up onto the near peaks.

In front of him and to the left, low on the slope, he could see the dark, square shapes of cattle grazing a mile and a half or so away. Uphill from the cattle—he was no judge, but there looked to be more cattle than the few hundred head Wheeler had mentioned bringing into the valley—he could see a small knot of other dark shapes closer to the line of trees that grew near but not in the valley. The small group was horses, also grazing and probably hobbled. Seen at this distance their dark outlines were rounded, where cattle have a square form when seen from afar.

Smith searched uphill from the horses until he found the small thread of smoke he was looking for. So some of Wheeler's men—he idly wondered how many the man had brought with him apart from the few Smith had already seen—were keeping an eye on the cattle.

That would be necessary, no doubt, until people in the valley had had time to adjust to the newcomers. Very few of the garden plots or small, cultivated fields in the valley had been fenced. There had never seemed any particular need for it before. Now that would change, and soon enough everything would have to be under fence.

Smith looked over his shoulder toward the bright emerald spears of his own oat crop and thought that he would have to fence it off too.

He spoke to the team and moved them slowly downhill with the weight of the wagon dragging against their breeching straps.

Aspen saplings, he thought as he drove. Lots of them. Whole saplings rather than split logs, he decided. They would replace themselves soon enough, and the work would be much quicker and easier that way. There certainly would be work enough involved without asking for more.

Post and rider construction, he decided. He wondered if a single rail would be enough to keep the cattle off his crop or if several would be necessary. Probably two. More work but more secure also.

He nodded to himself with satisfaction once that decision was reached, then felt of his pockets for his pipe. Two it would be.

Already he was planning which groves to take the trees from so the young growth would be thinned but not stripped.

CHAPTER 9

Smith pulled the wagon to a stop in front of Ben Frake's store, spoke to his team, then wrapped the lines around the empty whip socket. He never used a lash over his team and had not bothered to carry one with him since the team was broken. The thing had been gathering dust in a corner of his barn for years, ever since Jack and Jake were well started in harness. He reminded himself, though, to fetch it out one of these days for cleaning and oiling. There was no sense in owning something just to let it deteriorate. On the other hand, that was a reminder he gave himself at least once or twice a year. One of these days he would remember it when he was at home, and then he might actually get around to doing it.

He jumped down from the driving box and went through the routine, if unnecessary, precaution of clipping hitch weights to the bits of each horse, then went to the back of the wagon and dropped the tailgate so he could drag out the box of eggs he had brought. He had come in to see Asa Wheeler, but trips to town were not wasted.

He carried the crate inside and set it on the counter. There were no other customers in the store at the moment.

"Smith," Frake acknowledged with a nod. The storekeeper lifted the lid of the crate to peer inside. "Short box this time, I see. You been losing hens to the coyotes?"

"No. Had to come in anyway, so I thought I'd bring these by."

Frake nodded again and turned to go into the back of his store and bring out another, similar crate, empty except for sawdust. They had long ago arrived at the accommodation of keeping two crates for Smith's eggs, one to be delivered full and the other picked up empty for return. Smith never bothered to count the eggs that he sold to Frake. The storekeeper counted them when he had the time, calculated the amount that was owed and applied it to Smith's bill. It was a system that had worked out comfortably for both men for a number of years.

"Need anything while you're here, Smith?"

"No . . . yes. Come to think of it, I do. Fishhooks."

"All right." There was no need for Frake to ask what size. Smith always bought the same.

This time, though, Smith trailed behind him to the counter where small, wood-slab bins held hooks and sinkers and ready-made flies.

"Let me have a few of those too," Smith said. He pointed to a bin of hooks that were larger than his usual order, their tips barbed.

Frake raised an eyebrow. Smith had not bought a barbed hook in the storekeeper's memory and probably released many times more fish than he kept.

"For the girl," Smith explained. "She can't get the hang of a rod. I thought I'd see if I can teach her how to bait fish with a pole and bobber. It'd tickle her pretty good to be able to catch one her own self."

Frake smiled and counted out a dozen of the larger hooks and wrapped them separately in a twist of paper. "No charge for these, Smith."

"All right. Thank you."

The storekeeper used tongs to pick up a quantity of the hooks for Smith and weighed them on a small scale. It was easier—on the fingers especially—to sell them by weight rather than number. He weighed out an ounce of the tiny hooks, dribbled on a few extras and deposited them in another twist of scrap paper. Their price would be added to Smith's bill. "Anything else today?"

Smith shook his head. "I can't think of a thing."

"All right, then."

Smith dropped the two small packages of hooks into the egg crate he would be taking back with him and carried the box out to the back of the wagon. He latched the tailgate back into place and retrieved his hitch weights, depositing them on the floor of the driving box.

The Ramey house, the cowboy had said. Smith had to think for a moment to remember which one that would be. He was not used to visiting at any of the homes down here. In fact, he realized, this would make a first.

He grunted softly to himself, the sound barely audible as it escaped his throat. Surly, Tuck had said they called him down there.

And likely they did.

Not that Smith cared what they thought. Not anymore.

He arranged the driving lines between his fingers, taking his time about sorting and positioning them, then shook them slightly and clucked to the team. The big geldings took up the pull and moved out at a smart walk. By habit they began to turn back toward the rough track that led up to the house, and Smith had to correct them, guiding them downcreek toward the house that he thought was Ramey's.

CHAPTER 10

"Smith. *Good* to see you here. Thank you for coming." Wheeler had opened the door himself and was smiling broadly as he led Smith inside the house. If he was miffed because Smith had not come at once, several days ago when Tuck had delivered the message, he did not show it. He looked and sounded genuinely pleased that Smith had come.

Smith removed his hat and wiped his shoes carefully on the mat at the front door before he followed Wheeler inside. He looked from side to side, taking in the strange surroundings.

The house Wheeler had rented was about as nice as could be found in the valley, yet it was only a scant cut above Smith's rough cabin. The biggest difference was that the interior had been divided into several rooms, and of course it was larger. The furnishings, however, were little better than Smith's homemade articles. Pillows were used instead of upholstery on everything except for a none-too-clean overstuffed sofa in the parlor. The lamps were the kind that Frake sold in his store. Smith noticed several prints on the walls, none of them particularly well executed, and a handmade sampler that had been framed; it bore the simple message "Bless our home." Wheeler was obviously accustomed to wealth, but he made no apologies for the house. He guided Smith to a seat on the sofa, which was more comfortable than it looked, and for himself chose a hardwood rocker.

"Would you care for a drink, Mr. Smith? I have an excellent whiskey. Rye, I'm afraid. I didn't think to bring bourbon with me."

Smith shook his head. His expression was impassive, but the thought of a drink of whiskey pulled him in two directions. His stomach churned sourly in rejection of the idea, yet . . . He shuddered slightly. That had been a long time ago. "No, thank you."

"Something softer then? Lemonade? Coffee?"

"Nothing, thanks."

Wheeler looked beyond Smith to a doorway leading into the back of the house and shook his head. Smith turned in time to see that there was a woman standing there. He had not been aware of her until then. She must have come to the door after Smith came in. Certainly he would not have missed seeing her. She was attractive, buxom and quite young, twenty-five or possibly thirty years younger than Wheeler. She was dressed much too well to be a servant, but no introduction was made, as there almost certainly would have been if she were Wheeler's wife. She ignored Smith, nodded briefly toward Wheeler and disappeared into the back part of the house. She moved very quietly, Smith noticed. He had not heard her come and did not hear her leave.

"Taylor explained everything to your satisfaction, I trust," Wheeler said, getting straight to the point.

"He did. It occurred to me later that he made no mention of where the ditch, canal I believe he preferred to call it, would run after it leaves my property."

"But that would hardly be of interest to you, now would it?" Wheeler said smoothly. "You are satisfied as to where and how it will be constructed on your land?"

"Yes."

Wheeler smiled again. "Then all that remains is for you to sign the contract, and I shall pay you the thousand-dollar initial trespass fee." The big man sat back in the rocker and steepled his fingertips while he peered thoughtfully toward the ceiling. "This is, um, Thursday. I could wire my partners tonight and have them start the construction crew up on the morning train. Survey work could be completed over the weekend—our measurements and observation have been only tentative so far, of course, out of respect for your privacy—and the actual construction could begin first thing Monday morning. In fact, Mr. Smith, it occurred to me the other day"—he smiled again —"that we could spare ourselves some expense of transportation if we were to hire your team to pull the scraper. At, say, ten dollars a day if you have the time to drive them yourself, eight dollars daily if one of our men does it."

"Nobody else has ever driven that team," Smith said. The comment was only intended to buy him time to think. Ten dollars a day. Surely so much could not be the going rate even in the cities. There would have to be weeks of work involved. At ten dollars per day? And a thousand dollars, cash, just for allowing them to dig on his land? He had not seen that kind of money in . . . He *could* remember when. But he did not want to.

"That poses no problem, Mr. Smith. The choice is entirely yours, for your convenience."

Smith swallowed. He was still having some difficulty accepting the idea of so much money being suddenly available. Until this moment he had not really given all that much thought to it. Now, suddenly, it seemed real to him. Before Wheeler's offer had only seemed like so many words.

The thought of it was almost overwhelming and he found himself thinking about changing his mind and accepting Wheeler's offer of a drink as well. Just one, though. He could almost feel the warmth of it spread through his belly. It had been a very long time. And this time there was no answering churn of bile in rejection of the idea. The taste of it was very clear in his memory.

He opened his mouth to speak, ready to tell Wheeler that he would like a drink after all, but the big man was already rising to his feet.

"Let me get that paper for you to sign, Smith," Wheeler was saying. He winked at Smith. "And your trespass fee too, of course."

Wheeler walked quickly toward the back of the house. Smith sat alone in the small parlor. He closed his eyes for a moment and shuddered. No, damn it. He would not ask for that drink.

Wheeler was back after only moments out of sight. He had a leather folio in one hand and a thick wallet in the other. He laid the folio aside, opened the wallet and counted out coins. Small, glittering yellow coins the size and shape of twenty-five cent pieces. He counted them into piles of five, a hundred dollars to each pile, until he had ten stacks counted out. He pushed them together into one bright, tumbling mass and smiled at Smith. "There you are, Mr. Smith."

Smith ignored the money for the moment. "I haven't signed your contract yet, Mr. Wheeler."

Wheeler shrugged, retrieved the folio and opened it. He flipped several pages over until he came to the last one of the document, turned the folio so that the signature lines were presented to Smith and handed it to him. "There is pen and ink"—he looked around—"oh yes, over there. Let me get it for you." He fetched a steel nibbed pen and ink bottle and set them on the low table at Smith's elbow. "There you are." He was still smiling.

Smith laid the folio in his lap and turned the pages back to the beginning. There were four of them, written in that nearly incomprehensible jibberish that passes for English in courtrooms and writs.

The writing on the pages was quite small and had been done by machine. It was only the second time in Smith's life that he had seen machine-written words outside the pages of a book or periodical. He had to squint and hold the folio out farther to make out the words. The writing was rather pale against the cream of the heavy paper.

"Is there something you were looking for in particular? Perhaps I could help you."

"I haven't had time to read this before," Smith said. "Taylor forgot to bring it with him when he came up."

"Really? I hadn't known."

It was said quickly. Perhaps a bit too quickly. Smith was not sure that he believed it.

"I'll want to read it before I sign, of course."

"Of course," Wheeler said easily. "Are you sure you wouldn't like a drink, Mr. Smith?"

This time there definitely was no sense of revulsion at the idea. This time Smith positively yearned to accept the offer. Instead he shook his head quickly. Before he could change his mind. "No." He said it with too much force, too loudly and too fast. "No," he said again more calmly.

"Whatever you prefer, Mr. Smith." Wheeler smiled. "Of course."

Smith began to read the contract, slowly and thoroughly, taking his time to sift out the gist of meaning from among all the superfluous words.

CHAPTER 11

Smith straightened the pages carefully. It would have been almost criminal to crease the fine linen paper. Then he closed the folio with equal care and laid it aside.

"The pen—" Wheeler began.

"Yes. I know." He reached for his pipe and began to shave tobacco into it.

"You have some questions about the contract," Wheeler said. It was not a question.

"No," Smith said. "No questions." He smiled tightly. "An observation, perhaps, but no questions."

Wheeler's eyebrows went up.

"That contract gives you control of the gate," Smith said. He held his hand up before Wheeler could speak. "I know. The contract guarantees the integrity of my pond with minimum calculations given in feet of depth and acre-feet of storage." The thin smile reappeared briefly and then flickered away. "Frankly, sir, I would have to take your word on those. I've never measured the depth of my pond or the flow into it, and I'd have to go awfully far back into my memory to compute water volumes by acre-feet of storage. The point is, sir, that your people would have sole control of the flow. I would be specifically enjoined from manipulating the gates. That makes me curious, sir. And I notice that there is no mention of the water rights of downstream users. Under the terms of this contract, you would have full control and ownership of the water once it left my property line."

"But, Mr. Smith, surely you realize that any obligations on our part relating to downstream rights have no bearing on this contract. This document bears *only* on *your* water rights."

"You imply that there are other contracts, Mr. Wheeler, with the downstream users. Is that correct, sir? Are you prepared to contract with each of the downstream users?"

"Mr. Smith, surely that isn't your—"

Smith stood abruptly and extended his hand to Wheeler. "Thank you for your offer, sir, and good day."

"Mr. Smith, I truly think we can work something out that will satisfy . . ."

Smith was no longer listening. He turned and walked toward the door.

He thought of the drink Wheeler had offered, and this time there was once again the taste of bile in his throat as mind and stomach alike rejected it.

Wheeler was still talking, saying something to his back, but Smith had no interest in listening.

CHAPTER 12

He pulled the wagon to a halt and let the lines go slack. Jack and Jake stamped their feet and twitched, letting their heads sag gratefully. The load of green saplings was heavy work to pull, and the horses were sweating. The unexpected rest was welcome.

"There," Smith said. There was a note of discovery in his voice. Jack's left ear turned toward him at the sound, and Jake rolled one eye.

With a grunt of satisfaction Smith climbed down from the wagon box and bent low to the ground. He reached down and touched the top of a small, dark peg that had been driven into the ground.

"I'm sure of it," Smith said aloud. This time the horses did not react.

Ever since Taylor's visit, and especially so since he had spoken with Wheeler the second time, he had been curious about the markings Taylor would have made for the ditch course. There had to have been some. The man was, after all, an engineer. Taylor would not have dealt in abstract concepts or directions when he made his reports to Wheeler and the other partners in the canal venture. There would have to have been stakes placed and specific plans drawn.

Yet when he was here, Taylor had pointed out no markers for Smith to follow when he visualized the construction work.

There were no obvious stakes or flags anywhere along the planned watercourse.

Smith had wondered about that. And now he thought he had found the answer.

Instead of being tall, easily visible stakes with bright cloth or signboards attached, he had found a dark peg driven into the earth until its top was flush with the ground level.

He had noticed one earlier this morning on his way to the aspen stand and now another. It was only the square and therefore unnatural shape of the pegs that had brought them to his attention. But now he was fairly sure that he had found Taylor's markings.

He used his pocket knife to clear the earth away from the sides of the stake until he could get a grip on it with his fingers, then pulled it free. The peg was only six inches long, and its upper tip had been stained or painted to a color that nearly matched the soil into which it had been driven.

Damned odd, he thought. Stakes should normally be easy to spot. That was, after all, their purpose. To mark out a readily identifiable path.

Yet these were virtually hidden, by both color and size.

It seemed a remarkably curious thing for an engineer to have done.

He looked around while he reflected on that. He was standing now on his own property, very close to the south boundary of his land.

He sighted up toward the juniper where Taylor had said the ditch would run, then began looking along the ground in a direct line between the juniper and the empty hole from which he had just removed the marker.

From ground level it was impossible for him to see the next peg. If he had not virtually driven over the first one he never would have been able to see it, certainly would not have noticed it. He had to walk several steps toward the juniper before he found the second stake.

It too was dark-tipped and driven flush with the surface of the earth. It had been driven into the ground some five paces, call it fifteen feet, from the first.

"All right," he said aloud. "Five paces."

He turned and went back to the place where he had found the first peg and began following the canal course away from his land. He already knew where the ditch was intended to run on his property. He was still curious, though, about Wheeler's intentions elsewhere.

Smith was not a tracker, had never had to be, and it was slow going as he followed the curving ditch route off his land and onto the government land that Wheeler either controlled or had purchased—he was not quite clear about that either, come to think of it—more or less following the natural fall of the terrain.

Every fifteen feet, though, he was able to pick up the barely visible stub of another peg.

From the way both Wheeler and Taylor had talked, he would have expected the ditch to curve out barely onto the government land and then back again toward the original stream course.

Instead it continued out onto the dry grass flats that Wheeler controlled.

"Damned odd," Smith said aloud although by now the horses were much too far behind him to have heard. He loaded and lighted his pipe and then slowly, patiently went on, seeking out the now familiar square tops of the pegs.

They continued on, running parallel to the slope of the land now rather than falling with it. And now at every third marker there was a second peg driven beside the first. He had no idea what those second pegs signified.

He walked on like that for better than a quarter of a mile before he turned back. He still had no idea why the ditch route had been planned like that, or what the extra markers were intended to show, but he was sure that Wheeler intended for his canal to travel a considerable distance away from the original creek bed. The markers were leading farther and farther away from the stream, following a virtually flat course while the creek fell away with the slope of the valley floor until canal and creek were far apart.

Smith grunted to himself and stood for a moment with his arms folded, his eyes and memory trying to trace the ditch route back the way he had come, back to where his wagon stood waiting and beyond it, up the slope to the juniper that Taylor had pointed out to him.

There was no logic to the course that he could see. Certainly none the way the need and utilization had been explained to him.

If all Wheeler wanted was a ditch from which his cattle could be watered, why in the world would he spend additional money to dig it so far? A trough or a pond barely onto Wheeler's land would be enough to allow cattle to drink. If that was all the man wanted.

Smith grunted again. He drew on his pipe and heard a burble and hiss as the coal consumed the last of the tobacco. He knocked the bowl against his heel to empty the pipe, then stepped on the dottle, scattering it, to make sure the embers would not cause a fire.

Quickly now he began to hike back to his wagon. He had work to do and only so much daylight left in which to get it done.

CHAPTER 13

The old knife was thin, its edge a delicate feather. He had no idea how many times he had sat like this with the Arkansas stone in his lap, patiently and gently stroking it to achieve the edge he wanted. There was a certain pleasure in it, a certain satisfaction. He tested the edge on the hairs of his left forearm and, pleased with the result, laid the folding knife aside while he returned the stone to its wooden case. Like the knife blade, the whetstone had seen a great deal of use. Its dull gray surface was bellied in from years of service.

With the edge of his pocket knife renewed, Smith again picked up the dead and drying length of aspen and resumed his work on it.

Even when it was finished the pole would not have the action he wanted, but there were few native woods available in this high country, very few to choose from. It came down, really, to a choice between aspen and conifer. Even the ubiquitous cottonwoods had been left below. Few varieties of tree would grow at this altitude. Of those that would, none was really suited to fishing poles. Still, he would make do.

He continued to shave and to shape the aspen sapling he had chosen for the purpose. Finding just the right one had been difficult. A green, living sapling would have been much too supple and heavy, while a long dead one would have been dry and brittle. Eventually he had found this

one, partially dried and already as good as dead from a
porcupine's winter foraging.

It was not as straight as he would have liked, and the
butt section required a great deal of thinning to bring it
into an acceptable balance. Even with such a utilitarian
object as this, though, Smith wanted to make it as right as
he was able. Patiently he continued to strip away thin
slices of wood, shaping and rounding it to the hand as he
removed weight and thickness little by little.

He kept an eye on the shadows as he worked. He did not
want to be late.

Finally, satisfied at least for the moment, he folded the
knife closed and returned it to his pocket, then used a
length of scrap line to rig the pole for use. The barbed
hooks Frake had given him were already in his pocket, and
he had a selection of dry, two-inch-long limb sections in
his pocket as well, each of them with the bark removed
and a shallow groove whittled in a girdle around their
middles to accept the line and hold it fast. Cork bobbers
would have been nicer, but the dried wood ones were free
except for a few minutes of labor.

He picked up the box of grubs he had gathered earlier in
the morning, assembled his own more complicated gear
and began to walk up to the pond, glancing now and then
at the position of the sun to satisfy himself that he would
not be late. He always liked to arrive at the pond before
Susanna did. He had been late just once, and the girl had
been fretful and frightened. He did not want to put her
through that a second time.

Already he was planning how he would want to go
about teaching her.

Setting the hook once the bobber disappeared was the
important point he had to get across, and he was concerned about it.

She was excitable, and he knew she would be eager. She was likely to jerk the pole when she saw the bobber go under, and if she did it too forcefully she would tear the hook through the fish's mouth and lose her catch. The problem was how to explain it to her so she would pull with the right amount of force and not too quickly nor too late.

He wondered if she would understand if he told her to twitch the tip upward. Probably not. He pondered it while he walked, finally decided to instruct her to raise her arm after she saw the bobber dunk under. Raise it no faster than she would if she were waving goodbye to someone, the way she paused at the fringe of the timber every Sunday evening when she left him and stood there to wave goodbye.

That might work, he thought.

He mumbled a silent prayer as he walked, asking that Susanna learn to catch a fish of her very own this day.

It would please her so.

CHAPTER 14

"Smith."

"Come in." The sound of the voice in the night was no surprise. He had heard them come in. And if he had not, Joe had been there to warn him. He snapped his fingers, and the dog padded inside the house to take up a position at Smith's side. Joe relaxed on his haunches with his tongue out, enjoying the touch of Smith's hand on his ruff, so Smith assumed that Tuck was not out there. The dog seemed to dislike Tuck quite as much as Smith did.

It was Devore, the foreman, who came to the door. Smith thought he had heard more than one horse. He must have been mistaken.

"Help yourself to some coffee," Smith said. "It's on the stove there. Have you eaten?"

"Yes, but go ahead and finish your supper. You don't want it to get cold."

Smith looked at his visitor. He had more or less expected someone to come, Wheeler himself likely. Instead it was the foreman. Devore—he had to work at it to remember that the man's first name was Charles—seemed pleasant enough as a replacement for his employer.

Devore took a clean cup down from the shelf near the stove and poured a cup of coffee for himself, then sat in the chair opposite Smith's. His expression was open and amiable. Smith realized with some surprise that he could like this Charles Devore.

The man was tall and as lean as Smith but with no gray in his hair. Years of squinting against the glare of the sun had caused wrinkles at the corners of his eyes, and the back of his neck was burned nut-brown. He wore what seemed to be his habitual costume of boots, jeans, collarless shirt, vest and sleeve garters. His hat, which he dropped on the floor beside his chair, was broad-brimmed and crusted with sweat salt around the base of the rumpled crown.

Smith quickly finished his supper of fried eggs and trout while Devore waited patiently. There was silence between them, but it was comfortable. Smith felt no sense of strain or urgency in this man.

When he was done Smith scraped the bones and scraps from his meal into the bucket he would take out to the layers in the morning. The fish bones seemed a fair enough substitute for oyster shell or other forms of calcium for his laying flock, and he always fed them to his hens. He was not positive that they helped strengthen the shells of the eggs he got, but he believed that it was so.

He poured another cup of coffee for himself, freshened Devore's cup and sat down again.

Devore smiled. "I reckon you can guess why I'm here."

"Yes, I believe I can."

"Mind if I smoke?" Devore asked, breaking away from the subject he himself had broached.

"Go ahead." Smith pulled his pipe out while Devore took a cloth pouch of flake tobacco from his vest pocket and began to roll a cigarette.

Devore caught Smith looking at him curiously and smiled. "You never saw that before?"

Smith shook his head. "Heard of them. I don't believe I ever saw it done, though."

"Try one?" Devore offered the makings.

Smith shook his head again and continued to load his pipe. "This is good enough for me."

Devore finished rolling his smoke, licked it and accepted the light that Smith offered. "You never served around any Texans then, I'd say. Old habit down there. Seems to be catching on too."

"I see."

"Where did you serve?" Devore asked. "If you don't mind me asking."

"I—" Smith shook his head.

Devore seemed to take no offense at Smith's refusal to answer. He slouched down in the chair and blew a smoke ring toward the ceiling. "I was with Hood myself." He grinned. "A while back I'da been real upset at the thought of working for a bunch of damnyankees, but that was all a long time ago."

"A long time," Smith said. He wished he believed that. He shivered but thought he managed to hide it. "You don't look old enough to have been with Hood."

"I wasn't," Devore said easily. "I reckon none of us was, come to think of it. Or shoulda been. But I was there. Late, though. My big brother went first. Pap tried to, but they wouldn't let him. He had a stove-up leg from a bull that got to him when his horse went down in the brush. So they wouldn't let him sign up. My brother Tom went from our family, an' when he was killed it was my turn. Pap went with me to sign me in. Tried to join up himself again, but they still wouldn't let him. So he signed for me to go. It was after Vicksburg. They tell me I'm lucky." A haunted frown tugged at the corners of his mouth. "Maybe they're right. I wouldn't know."

A shiver rolled up Smith's spine again, but he said nothing. Vicksburg. Lord God, Vicksburg. Devore had indeed been fortunate. Devore had not been at Vicksburg.

"What does Wheeler want?" Smith asked, changing the subject back. It was too late, though. The night dreams would come again. He knew they would. He could already feel a thin, oily film of sweat break out on his forehead. He almost wished that just this once he would remember the dreams when they woke him. Perhaps that way he could face them and end them.

Devore looked at him curiously, then nodded. Smith knew the man did not understand, not really, but he tried to and probably thought that he did. His sympathy was genuine enough. Smith appreciated it.

"He wants to up the ante," Devore said. "He'll pay fifteen hundred for starters and a hundred fifty every year."

"I didn't refuse to sign just to get more money from him," Smith said softly.

"I didn't reckon you did." Devore inspected the tip of his cigarette instead of looking at Smith. He tapped a length of ash into his palm.

"Use the floor. It's all right. I sweep every night before I go to bed anyway."

"If you're sure."

"I am."

Devore turned his hand over, allowing the clot of loose ash to drift down to the floor.

"Why do those markers go so far out?" Smith asked. "And what are those extra pegs for?"

Devore looked at him and shrugged. "If I knew, Smi— Mind if I call you Stillwater? Smith seems awful impersonal somehow."

"I don't mind."

"All right then, Stillwater. If I knew, I'd tell you. And that's the natural truth. But I don't. Mr. Wheeler and that Taylor fella don't say so much to me, you understand. Not about their plans. I don't know much about how money

works. I know cows." He smiled. "If I knew more about
the other, I reckon I'd be keeping cows of my own 'stead
of nursemaiding them for some other fella. I know how to
pack tallow under their hides and how to move them from
one place to another without losing more of it than you
have to, and that's about it. And that's about all they ask
me about or tell me to do. But what their plans are?" He
shook his head. "I expect you'd know more about that
than I do."

Smith smiled at him. "Then we're both in the dark."

Devore grinned. "I been there before, Stillwater. I expect you have too."

Smith chuckled. That was the truth. And by Godfrey, if
he had anything to drink in the house he would have offered something to Charles Devore. He had not felt that
way toward anyone in a very long time.

"Well, Charles, you can tell Mr. Wheeler that you delivered his message."

"Charlie," Devore corrected. "Nobody but Wheeler and
that Taylor fella ever calls me Charles."

"All right, Charlie. You can tell him."

Charlie grinned. "Coulda saved myself the trip, I
reckon, but that wouldn't have been right, would it?"

"No. I, uh, don't suppose Wheeler mentioned any
change in who was to have the key to the gates. That's
what I object to, not the money."

"No, he never said nothing about that. Just the money.
That's—" He changed his mind about whatever he had
been about to say and closed his mouth again with a slight,
annoyed shake of his head.

He did not have to finish it. Smith understood. And
understood as well that as long as Charlie Devore was
taking Asa Wheeler's pay, Charlie would not say anything
that might be critical of his boss.

"More coffee, Charlie?"

Devore grinned. "I'd like that, Stillwater. Thankee."

Smith got up to refill both their cups, and Joe flopped loudly down to the floor. The dog's tail beat a dull, slow rhythm against the leg of Smith's chair.

CHAPTER 15

He bent and plucked an errant weed from among the many thin, emerald stalks of the young oats. He threw the weed stem away and smoothed down the soil where the roots had been drawn up.

Still hunkered low to the ground, he picked up a handful of earth and crumbled it in his fingers. The soil was dark and friable, watered from beneath the surface by underground seepage from the creek and kept loose by his careful tillage. It was good ground, very nearly as good as any he had seen anywhere, although just a matter of a few rods away, farther up the slope away from the stream, the soil was pale and dry and hard. The narrow strip of bottom was marvelously rich, the hillsides so close virtually barren. The contrast never ceased to amaze him.

Smith stood and bent backward to take the kinks out of his spine. He was beginning to feel his age, he reflected.

Still, this was a good life he had chosen. The work was hard, but he felt rewarded by it.

The strain of early oats he had planted was already springing eight, nine inches high. Within a month the stalks would begin to head, setting seed that would provide his winter feed. And provide him as well with straw for bedding and roughage.

At this time of year, with the crop green and promising, the oats were a real joy. That too never ceased to amaze him. Farming was not exactly what he had expected. It pleased him to realize how much he enjoyed it.

A hint of smile thinned his lips as another thought came to him.

In another few months he would not be so pleased with it all.

Then, with the crop matured and drying on the stalks, it would be time to drag out the scythe and cradle and harvest the damned things.

That was something he never had learned to enjoy. And was not likely to at this late date.

The threshing and winnowing were not so bad. It could be done slowly, almost at leisure once the stalks were cut and stacked and put under cover.

But the cutting. Damn the cutting.

Backbreaking, arm-wrenching, hot, dusty, sweat-sticky work from first light to last. Swinging that scythe and the heavy wooden cradle tines laboriously back and forth. Sweep and step and sweep and step, mowing the field by hand one slow swath after another.

Then his few acres seemed to occupy the entire valley and for endless miles beyond.

Smith thought wistfully of the money Asa Wheeler had offered. Until this moment it had not occurred to him, but with that kind of cash in his pocket he could afford to order one of those mowing machines. Could let Jack and Jake do the work of the cutting while he rode on a steel sulky seat. The damned scythe and cradle could be hacked up for stovewood. And wouldn't he enjoy *that* fire. It would warm him through and through.

Amusement with himself crinkled the corners of his eyes, and Smith nearly laughed out loud.

He took another look around at the flat, green expanse of young oats.

He had never bothered to calculate just how much land he had under crop, but a rough, eyeball guess put it in the neighborhood of fourteen acres give or take a bit.

And for fourteen acres he was going to spend more than three hundred dollars to buy a mower?

He chuckled softly to himself.

Of course the mower would be as useful for making hay as for cutting grain.

The thought sneaked in almost of its own volition.

And then what? Smith asked himself. Sit around and get fat?

That thought amused him too. He looked down at the flat, sunken belly behind his belt and shook his head. With a grin he tried to imagine himself at Asa Wheeler's bulk. He could not do it. The idea seemed much too farfetched.

Get like that, he thought, and he would likely have to hitch the team just to go up to the pond. Or get there puffing and wheezing as Taylor had done that day.

He found that idea funny too.

Smith sighed and fought back a grimace. All right, damn it. The truth was that he *would* like to own a mowing machine.

And those spectacles that he was beginning to need.

And . . . His frown turned into a wry grin. Why not a racehorse too? Or a surrey. Maybe a mansion on a hill, with white fences and magnolias and dogwood and azalea plantings.

Sure. Why not all of that.

Abruptly the grin faded and was replaced by a blank, faraway stare of haunted pain.

A chill ran through him, and he shuddered. The sun no

longer felt good on his shoulders, and he took no more pleasure in the sight of his growing crop.

He turned and walked blindly toward the house, wishing that that damned Joe were somewhere about.

CHAPTER 16

It took him a moment to recognize her. He had only seen her from a distance before or in passing on the street and then not often. She kept to herself as a rule, as he did also.

And the times he had seen her before she had looked much better than she did now.

Now she was disheveled and nervous. She came up the path at a slow, stumbling trot, her face flushed, eyes darting from side to side. She was limping a little and might have fallen, and she hurried forward with the front of her skirt clutched in both hands and raised slightly to ease her progress. He was able to see part of her calf above the ankles but pretended that he did not because he did not want to embarrass her.

"Mrs. Guynon." He removed his hat and bobbed his head, then put down the posthole digger he had been using, trying to ring his oat field with aspen posts ready for the fencing he would have to put in.

The woman was laboring for breath. She stopped in front of him, feet wide apart, and had to wait several moments before she could speak.

"Mr.—" She gasped for air and had to try again. "Mr. Smith. Have you seen Susanna?"

Her worry was contagious. "No, I haven't, ma'am."

"She's—" The woman gulped in another breath and hurried on. "She's disappeared. I sent her . . . on an errand. For eggs. We needed three eggs. For a recipe. But

Mr. Frake." She was breathing too quickly now, trying to compensate. "He hasn't seen her. I thought. She might have come here. To you. For the eggs?"

It was no secret in the valley where Ben Frake bought his eggs. There were few enough hens anyway, and Smith was the only one to keep them who produced much more than his own needs would require.

It was probably no secret either, Smith reflected, that the child was fond of him.

"You haven't seen her, Mr. Smith?" Susanna's mother sounded better, no calmer now but at least able to breathe again.

"No, ma'am, I haven't. But I'd be glad to help you look for her. How long has she been gone?"

"I don't— Let me think. An hour. More? I'm not sure."

"Time enough for you to become worried and go all the way down to town and then back up here on foot?" Afoot that would have meant a time lapse of three, four hours or even more.

"No, I saw Mr. Frake on the road. He was coming up from town. He hadn't passed Susanna."

"Good," Smith said gently. "She couldn't have gotten into all that much trouble in an hour or so, could she?" He was not sure he believed that himself, but he wanted the woman to calm herself.

Instead Mrs. Guynon began to cry.

"Why don't you go into my house. The door's open. Sit down and get your breath, ma'am. I'll run up to the pond and see if she stopped up there before she came to ask for the eggs." He smiled. "She likes it up there, you know. She might've come by and saw that I wasn't at the house and just, well, wandered on up to the pond."

The woman nodded. She looked a mess. Her hair was coming down, and her face was puffed and blotchy. Smith

offered his arm but she did not seem to see, so he took her
gently by the elbow and guided her up to the house.

Once she was inside and out of view, though, he turned
and broke into a shambling run up to the pond. He was
more worried than he wanted Mrs. Guynon to know.
Susanna would not likely be able to cope with any unexpected difficulties.

As he ran he prayed that he would find her there,
perched on Smith's favorite rock perhaps and watching for
a trout to break water or rise to an insect.

Let it be so, he asked as he ran.

CHAPTER 17

"I want you to drive down to town, Mrs. Guynon. Maybe she stopped to play with some children, something like that. I want you to look for her there. I've already hitched the team for you. You can drive, can't you?"

She nodded. Her expression was dull and empty from the sustained fear.

"All right then. You look for her there. I'll go up in the trees and look for her there. You know how she likes to walk up there and look at the birds." He tried to smile. "Why, she might have seen a wild canary. She might be trying to follow it to its nest and just went and forgot what you told her to do."

Mrs. Guynon's face twisted. She almost began to cry again but managed to control herself. "She would not have forgotten, Mr. Smith. Susanna is very conscientious, you know. When I give her a task she can do, she is always so pleased to be able to help that she concentrates on nothing else."

Smith smiled and touched her shoulder lightly. "All children can be forgetful, Mrs. Guynon."

The woman sighed and stood. "We aren't accomplishing anything here."

"No, ma'am, we aren't," Smith agreed. Mrs. Guynon sounded calmer now, more in control. He was pleased.

He was also, though, increasingly worried about Susanna. It was not like the girl to disappear like this.

He helped Mrs. Guynon onto the wagon and was pleased to see that she handled the lines competently. It annoyed him to discover that he was concerned now about his team as well as about Susanna. There was no excuse for that. The safety of the child was more important than any number of horses, and realizing his concern for Jack and Jake in the hands of a stranger made him feel small.

"Godspeed, ma'am."

The woman nodded and shook the lines to put the team into motion. The horses pulled for her without hesitation, and she drove at a fast trot down the path toward town. Smith turned and hurried across the creek and up into the timber, toward the faint path that Susanna used when she walked up for their every-Sunday-afternoon fishing.

Smith wished that he were more of a woodsman, that he knew something about tracking. All he could do now was look and hope and try to find her.

"Hello."

Smith jumped. The unexpected voice came from his left. He had just looked in that direction but had seen nothing. In his concentration in searching for Susanna he had managed to completely overlook a man sitting in shadowed but quite open view on the back of a short-coupled horse.

Smith looked again and blinked as man and horse came into clear focus. The rider was Wheeler's cowhand Bill, sitting with one knee crooked over the horn of his saddle and cigarette makings cupped in his hands.

"Mr. Smith, right?"

Smith nodded and walked toward him.

The cowboy finished rolling his smoke, lighted it and held the small sack of tobacco out toward Smith. "Care for some?"

"No, thanks. Have you seen anything of a girl today? Lost perhaps?"

Laugh wrinkles deepened at the corners of Bill's eyes. "A girl you say? Now I'm right sure I'd recall it if I ran into a pretty girl up here. Or any other kind, come to that." He became more serious. "She's lost, you say?"

"I don't know that," Smith explained. "Not for sure. But she's missing, and her mother is worried."

"Little girl? Big one? What?"

"It's the child you and that friend of yours were talking about the first time I saw you."

"Oh." Bill looked embarrassed. "The one that ain't quite right in the head."

"That's right."

"I ain't . . . I mean I haven't been bothering her. If that's what you were thinking, Mr. Smith."

The thought quite frankly had not occurred to Smith. Not until now. Now it alarmed him, and he looked at Bill more closely.

The cowboy looked troubled and concerned but not guilty, Smith conceded. He put his cigarette makings back into his shirt pocket and shifted his leg off the horn so that he was sitting the horse properly again.

"I'd sure like to help you look for her, Mr. Smith," Bill said. "That's what I'm doing here anyway. Not looking for her, I mean, but for one of our riders. Tuck. You seen him in the store that time. He wandered off somewheres this afternoon, likely taking himself a snooze under a tree someplace, and the foreman's kinda pissed about it. He sent me to find 'im and get him back where he belongs. So I reckon I can look for that girl while I'm lookin' for him too."

"I'd appreciate that, Bill."

"Sure thing, Mr. Smith." He grinned. "Ol' Charlie

passed the word that we was supposed to be nice to you anyhow. Said the big boss wants you buttered up for some reason. So I reckon I'd get in some trouble if I didn't offer to help you."

Smith smiled and would have responded. He stopped, though, when he saw a troubled look cross Bill's eyes. "What is it, Bill?"

"You don't reckon . . . ? Naw."

"What?"

Bill shook his head and would not answer.

"Tuck?" Smith guessed.

"He ain't a bad fellow, Mr. Smith. Really he ain't. I don't think he'd do a thing like that. Not after you explained it to us an' everything."

"Do you know where he is, Bill?"

"No, sir. Not really. But I found some tracks that're likely his. That's what I been following up through here." Bill pointed toward the ground, but Smith could not see anything there that remotely resembled a hoof- or footprint to him. There were a few shallow scrapes in the soil among the rocks that covered the rising hillside among the trees, but if those were the tracks that Bill had been following they defied Smith's interpretation.

"I think if you don't mind, Mr. Smith, I'll be getting on with what I was doing."

Smith nodded, and Bill reined his horse uphill and began to ride in a winding, slow route.

On an impulse Smith began to hike up the hill behind the horse.

He was feeling more worried now than he had since Mrs. Guynon had first approached him.

CHAPTER 18

Fortunately for Tuck, Bill got there first on the strength and stamina of the little horse. Smith was lagging a good sixty yards behind, puffing and panting despite his physical condition and years-long acclimatization to the altitude. Smith had to force himself up the final grade, a deep, sickened anger giving him the strength for it.

Tuck seemed actually pleased to see his friend. He certainly showed no indications of shame or embarrassment even though Susanna was on the ground nearby, huddled against a boulder and crying softly.

Bill stepped off his horse and let the reins fall to the ground. The animal sidestepped nervously away, probably sensing the tension from its rider. Tuck stood and grinned at his friend. "Your turn, bu—"

Bill's fist lashed out, catching Tuck flush on the mouth and driving him backward. His spur caught on a low rock, and he tripped, falling backward and sprawling to the ground.

"What the hell?"

Bill silently motioned for Tuck to get up. When he did, Bill knocked him down again.

"Now just a damn minute here." Tuck came to his knees, gathered himself and threw himself at Bill.

Smith, finally reaching the little rock-rimmed bowl where Tuck had been having his afternoon fun, ignored both of them and stumbled the last few yards to Susanna's side.

He knelt beside the weeping girl, pulling her to him to cradle her head against his chest and rock her gently back and forth while he petted her hair and patted her and tried to soothe away some of her fear and confusion.

Her dress was rumpled but untorn, and there were no obvious bruises or abrasions on her. None, at least, that he could see. She was frightened, though, and it took him a little while to calm her.

Tuck was over his surprise now and fighting back. Tuck was the shorter of the two but probably the heavier also. He swung a roundhouse right. Bill ducked under it and pummeled Tuck in the stomach with a flashing series of lefts and rights, then darted away again as Tuck tried to kick him.

Smith turned Susanna's head so that she could not see. She was already upset enough and probably could not understand why the two cowboys were fighting anyway.

"You're all right now, honey. Everything is going to be all right now," Smith crooned to her. He said it softly, directly into her ear, hoping it would distract her from the sound of grunts of effort and the dull thudding of fists meeting flesh and the scrape of bootheels against gravel.

"The man said we'd have fun," Susanna wailed in a thin, quavering voice, "but we didn', Stillwater. We didn' have fun, Stillwater. It *hurt.*" Her eyes were wide. "And it wasn't fun. He said it would be, but it wasn't fun."

"I know, baby. I know." Smith cupped her head in his hands, holding her close against him, and rocked her back and forth. "I know, honey."

"Get up, you son of a bitch." Bill's voice was harsh and tight. He stood with his feet planted wide, and his fists balled. Tuck was on the ground. Blood seeped from his mouth and the corner of one eye and was flowing freely from his nose. He shook his head.

"Get up," Bill hissed.

"You're the one—"

"That's right, an' we both found out different too. But you couldn't leave it be, could you, you son of a bitch. Now get up an' get out of here. The foreman wants you anyhow, though why anybody would want you around is more'n I can figure. Jesus, man. Word o' this gets around, and there won't none of us be welcome here. An' I couldn't blame nobody for it but you. Now git. G'wan. Git!"

Tuck dragged himself to his feet and paused only long enough to give Smith and Susanna a murderous glance. Then he stumbled toward his horse, tied to a tree nearby.

It took him two attempts to make it into his saddle, and then he had to hang on to the horn to help lift himself into it.

He gave Bill a look that was as hard as the one he had given to Smith and the girl, then reined the animal downhill and started away.

Bill looked at Smith. His expression was pained and embarrassed. He opened his mouth, but no words came out. After a moment he shook his head sadly and turned to pick up the trailing reins of his still fidgety mount.

Smith nodded to him. He continued to hold on to Susanna, petting and stroking the back of her head. Her crying had subsided. She was only sniffling every once in a while now.

He sighed and eased down to the ground beside her. He would give her a few more minutes to calm down. Then they would have to begin the long walk back.

Smith was already worrying about what he would have to say to her mother when they got back.

CHAPTER 19

"No one must know, Mr. Smith. We mustn't let *any*one know about this."

"I understand how you feel, Mrs. Guynon. The embarrassment—"

"No," she said sharply. "You don't understand at all." She gave him a stricken look, her eyes bright with tears not yet shed. "What frightens me is that . . . the way some people, some men . . . are . . . they might think . . . I mean now that the damage has been done . . . they might . . ."

"Oh." Smith had honestly not thought of that. But she was right. The way some people were, particularly some men whose views could be twisted for the sake of their own convenience, she was right. There would be some who would undoubtedly decide that the whole, awful affair had been Susanna's fault.

And they would use that view to justify other, similar incidents in the future.

He shuddered. Susanna, trusting and simple, would never be able to defend herself. Neither with words nor physically. The thought of it made him sick.

He sat at the Guynon table, a cup of water untouched in front of him, and glanced toward the closed door where Mrs. Guynon had put Susanna to bed a little while before. She was sleeping quite soundly now, her mother said, apparently unconcerned any longer about what had hap-

pened to her. Before her mother bathed her and put her to
bed she had seemed completely over the experience, probably unable to retain it. Smith had never thought of her
affliction as being any kind of a blessing, but perhaps at
this moment it was. She seemed to have no thoughts or
memories to haunt her.

Smith took another look around the crude house. It had
been stoutly built and stoutly furnished, but that must
have been when Phil Guynon was still alive.

Smith had never met the man. He knew Guynon had
come here as a tie cutter when the railroad was being built.
He had brought his family with him and installed them in
this cabin. Then there had been an accident, a log chain
breaking or something of that nature—Smith had never
heard the details and did not particularly want to—and
the wife had been left a widow. For some reason she had
stayed on with Susanna.

How she managed to make a livelihood for the two of
them, Smith did not know.

Now that he had seen the inside of their home, though,
he realized for the first time just how welcome it must have
been whenever he sent fish home with Susanna.

He sighed, thinking back. It had been—how long now—
a year? Possibly longer than that. He could not remember.

Always he had enjoyed his pond. From the very beginning it had been his place of refuge and pleasure. Then last
spring, he guessed it had been, he started finding footprints
along the bank. And there had from time to time been a
sense that someone was watching him when he was at the
pond. The sense had been especially strong on Sunday af-
ternoons.

It had taken him weeks to realize that he was being
watched from the timber, from across the pond from his
favorite rock. It had taken him more weeks to find out

who was watching him. The child had been as shy as a doe. Yet once she knew she had been seen there, she came to him with all the open, eager friendliness of a guileless puppy.

She accepted him completely, without reservation of any kind, and there had been no way he could have failed to respond to her, even if he had wanted to. It surprised him to realize that he enjoyed her company quite as much as she seemed to enjoy his.

Since then it had become an every-Sunday meeting. It had become something he looked forward to all the week long. He hoped that sense of pleasure would not be diminished now.

Smith sighed again. Lord knew, he had never really thought about Susanna's physical maturity. He did not know—*she* did not know—but he guessed she was seventeen, possibly eighteen years old now. Her body was certainly that of a woman grown. Funny that he had not consciously realized that until Bill and that damned Tuck had come along. He always thought of her as being a child, which truly she was. She spoke and moved and acted the way he would imagine a child of five or six should speak and move and act.

He hoped that innocence would not be destroyed now.

Smith looked back at her mother. "Do you want me to talk to the men at the cow camp, Mrs. Guynon? I happen to know the foreman. I could . . . explain to him. If you like."

She nodded. "I would appreciate that, Mr. Smith. In my heart I wish the good Lord would send down a bolt of lightning to strike that young man dead. I do, sin though that is for vengeance belongs to the Lord and not to me. But for Susanna's sake, I would like you to talk to them. No one must know, Mr. Smith. For her sake."

"Yes, ma'am."

He was beginning to feel uncomfortable and wanted to leave, but common courtesy dictated that he remain and drink the cup of water she had given him. He suspected that it had been offered because she had nothing else to give. Coffee and tea were both expensive luxuries. Which Smith had not really considered before. He thought of himself as a frugal man with few needs and fewer expenses, yet he took for granted the purchase of coffee now and then. It was only in comparison with Susanna and her mother that he realized the extent of his own wealth. He wondered if Mrs. Guynon would resent a suggestion from him that an acceptably pleasing tea could be made from the bark of the junipers that grew in clumps on the mountainsides.

Not now, he decided. He would gather some for them and send it home with Susanna at some time in the future, possibly with a note to explain where it came from. He could word the note as an apology rather than a suggestion and avoid giving offense or wounding the woman's pride.

She certainly must have a great deal of pride to be able to cope with the lot that had been given her.

Smith sipped his water and smiled and spoke softly of inconsequentials for a time. Then, relieved, he excused himself and went out to collect his team and wagon.

He would have to find Devore's camp immediately and have that talk, he realized. Charlie would understand. He felt sure of that.

This was turning out to be a much longer and harder day than he had expected.

CHAPTER 20

Devore's greeting was jarring, to say the least.

When Smith drove up to the camp, Charlie Devore stood with a broad, welcoming grin and motioned him toward the campfire where a blue-enameled coffeepot was sitting at the side of the coals.

Charlie acted as if nothing at all unpleasant had happened with him or any of his men. It did not seem right. Certainly it was not what Smith would have expected if he understood Charlie Devore anything like as well as he thought he did.

"Come to find out what good meat tastes like, Stillwater?" Devore asked cheerfully. "Tell me how many extra steaks you want thrown on the fire, and pull up a rock then."

"No, uh . . . That isn't what I had in mind." Smith was confused. Surely there had been more than enough time for Charlie to have been fully informed about what had happened.

He looked around as he climbed down from the wagon and reached inside for his hitch weights. There were four saddled horses tied to a picket rope strung between two firs. Devore and another man had been sitting near the fire. Tuck and a fourth man were beyond the fire, kneeling over a canvas-wrapped haunch of fresh beef. Obviously the crew was preparing their evening meal.

There was no sign of Bill.

"Where's your other man?" Smith asked. "Bill something-or-other." If he had ever heard Bill's last name he could not now recall it.

Devore took one of the hitch weights from him and clipped it to Jake's bit while Smith tended to Jack. He gave Smith a guarded look and lowered his voice. "Do you know anything about that, Stillwater?"

"About what?" Smith felt more confused than ever at the question.

" 'Bout Bill, that's what. Tuck came ridin' in here a little bit ago looking like he'd been in a helluva fuss. Told me the old man's fired Bill out from under me an' gave him his wages, so I wouldn't be seeing him no more. Said Bill was already on his way outa the valley."

"The old man would be Wheeler?"

"Ayuh. Kinda puts me in a bad spot, though. He's never mixed in with my business before this. I got no idea what prompted him to do it now except that Tuck must've had something to do with it."

"Why should Tuck have anything to do with it?"

"I guess there wouldn't be any reason for you to know, at that. Tuck's Asa's nephew. His sister's youngest, I think it is."

"I'll be damned," Smith muttered. He followed Charlie to the fire and accepted the cup of steaming, long-boiled coffee that Charlie handed him.

Smith was still trying to get his thoughts in order. He started to speak but was interrupted by the outbreak of a loudly squealing kicking match between two of the horses on the picket line. Devore rushed over to separate them and get them calmed down.

Tuck took the opportunity to sidle over to the fire and hunker beside it. He fed a few chunks of dry wood unnecessarily onto the coals. Out of the corner of his mouth, without once turning his head to look at Smith, he hissed, "You say anything about what happened this afternoon, you son of a bitch, and I'll get you. You understand me, old man?"

Smith was unimpressed by the cowboy's threat, but before he could tell him so Tuck moved away. Devore was on his way back to the fire. He grinned and shook his head.

"Sorry about that, Stillwater, but you know how it is. Every horse ever borned is a nitwit."

"Like some people," Smith muttered.

Charlie thought he was making a joke. He began to chuckle.

That explained Charlie's unconcerned friendliness when he approached, Smith realized. The foreman of the cow camp did not know what his man had done.

Didn't know why another of his men had been fired either.

Lordy.

It presented Smith with a dilemma. He had come here to ask Charlie not to talk about the incident. Well, he sure could not talk about something that he did not know about.

But, dammit, he *should* know. Smith did not want him to *do* anything about it. Save for firing Tuck, that is, which he obviously could not do if he wanted to. Not with Tuck being close kin to Asa Wheeler.

If Smith said anything about it now, he would not only make it likely that word would get around about what had happened to Susanna, he would also very likely cost Charlie Devore his job. He doubted very strongly that a man like Charlie Devore would stay on as foreman with a crew over whom he had no control, nor would he be willing to knowingly have anyone like John Friar as a member of that crew.

But if Smith kept his mouth shut about this afternoon, he would not really be doing Charlie any favors.

Worst of all—and it graveled him badly—if he kept quiet about it, Tuck would believe that Stillwater Smith had backed down to the young fool's threats.

It was that thought that made Smith's decision for him.

Any decision to speak up might be weighted by Smith's own pride, by his refusal to knuckle under to Tuck's threats.

A decision to remain quiet would be solely for Susanna's benefit and protection.

Damn the man, though, Smith thought. He glared across the fire toward where Tuck was piling steaks onto a piece of oilcloth. Tuck saw the look and began to laugh. The little bastard had gotten away with it.

Bile roiled bitterly in Smith's throat and stomach, and it was all he could do to force down a sip of the coffee Devore had given him.

"You never said how many steaks you can handle," Charlie said pleasantly, unaware of the tensions around him.

"None," Smith said. "I mean . . . thanks . . . but I can't stay. I have some chores to finish up at home before it gets too dark."

"Well, I wish you'd change your mind, Stillwater, but you know what you gotta do. Any time, though. You don't need an invitation to any fire of mine."

"Thanks, Charlie. I appreciate that." Smith dumped out the rest of his coffee, set the cup down and went back to his wagon. If he did not get away from the camp now he was going to do things that he would regret later. Memory washed coldly through him, and he shuddered.

No, he swore to himself as he threw the hitch weights hurriedly into the back of the wagon and swung the team downhill toward home.

Never again.

CHAPTER 21

The clamshell-shaped head of the posthole digger dropped into the hole with a dull, low thump, biting into the rich soil of its own weight. Which was considerable. By this time of day Smith felt all too well the weight of it. Still, the work was progressing. One slow post at a time. He pried the long handles apart, trapping a small quantity of earth between the twin blades, and lifted, setting the tool beside the hole and pulling the handles together again to spill out the dirt he had just removed. He checked the daub of mud he had smeared onto one handle to mark the depth. A few more and this one should be deep enough, he decided. Two and a half feet per post. He would allow himself no less.

Sweat trickled a tickling path down his sides, and he paused for a moment to wipe it off his forehead and away from his eyes, then once again dropped the digger into the hole. He heard the solid, chunky thud as the head bit and a thin, higher-pitched scrape as a blade shaved past a buried rock. At least that was a blessing, he thought. There was little stone in this loamy bottom land. The work would have been considerably harder upslope where the earth was hard and heavy and laden with rock that had eroded off the mountainsides.

He finished the hole and laid the posthole digger aside to pick up one of the thick post sections he had cut, upended the sapling butt section and dropped it into the hole. He picked up his tamper, the broken handle of an old peavey, and began kicking dirt back into the hole, using the hardwood prod to pack the loose dirt tight around the newly set pole so it would be firm in the ground when he was done. The young oats were sure to be a temptation to Wheeler's cattle, and he did not want to make it easy for them to push his fence over. He had no idea how long Wheeler expected to close-herd the cattle, but he doubted the man would be willing to spend money for extra manpower indefinitely.

Smith finished with that post, picked up his tools and moved along a measured eight feet to the next post location. With a sigh he wiped his forehead again and stared accusingly at the virgin ground at his feet. This was not exactly the way he had planned to spend his fat and easy time of the year.

A sound to his rear made him turn. Two horsemen were approaching. He recognized the fine Cleveland Bay that Wheeler rode. The bulk of the man on it would have to be Wheeler himself. They were still far enough away that he could not tell who was with the former major.

Smith grunted to himself and bent to pick up the water bottle he had carried down to the field with him. The water was sun-warmed and tepid. Since his work was being interrupted anyway another minute or so would hardly matter. He poured the warmish water onto the ground and walked down to the creek to refill the bottle with fresh water cold from the stream bed. That was better. He drank deeply of it, then tilted the bottle over his shoulders to let the cooling fluid rush over his chest and back. He could hardly get any wetter than sweat had already made him, and the chill feel of it was refreshing. Then he stooped to refill the bottle again.

He nodded a welcome of sorts as Wheeler and Tuck—Charlie Devore was not with them—reached the creek.

Their horses stopped there for a moment to toss their heads and survey the crossing, then splashed through the cold-running water to the side of the creek where Smith had been working.

"Mr. Smith. Good day, sir." Wheeler spoke with a hearty enthusiasm. Tuck fidgeted in the background, his eyes averted from Smith's glare.

"Mr. Wheeler," Smith grudgingly acknowledged. He continued to stare at John Friar.

After a moment Tuck got his courage up. And his anger. He stared back at Smith, eyes narrowed in unspoken challenge. Smith looked from one man to the other but was unable to decide if Wheeler had been told the truth about what had happened the other day. If so he was certainly able to hide it well, for he showed no hint of embarrassment or uneasiness now.

"I expect you know why I've come to see you, Mr. Smith," Wheeler said. "Devore told me he delivered my message."

"He did," Smith said. "I assume he returned with mine."

Wheeler smiled easily. No, Smith decided. He must not have been told. The man could not possibly be as brazen as all that with one of his kin a molester of children.

"I was hoping we could discuss it further, Mr. Smith," Wheeler said. "Face-to-face and man-to-man, as it were. Surely we can arrive at some accommodation. I am, uh, willing to be as generous as I possibly can. Although of course you will realize that our investment funds are not, uh, unlimited."

"It isn't the money," Smith said softly. His attention was more on Tuck than on Wheeler.

Wheeler glanced back at his nephew, then at Smith again. Awkwardly and with some difficulty, certainly with none of the fluid grace displayed by Devore and Tuck and the other cowboys who lived and worked with their horses, Wheeler disengaged his handsome boot from the off stirrup, swung his leg heavily over the saddle and lowered himself to the ground. He looked grateful to have solid earth underfoot again and wheezed a little as Tuck sprang down from the back of his cow pony and hurried to take the reins from Wheeler's hand.

"May I have a drink?" Wheeler asked.

"Of course." Smith reached for the cork stopper of his water bottle, but Wheeler did not see. The big man turned and went to the creek. He pulled a flat object from his coat pocket and shook it. It was a collapsible cup made of bright metal, probably silver. It had been a long time since Smith had seen a cup like that, although once they had enjoyed a certain popularity and were almost a standard article among the personal kits of the wealthier officers.

Wheeler had to kneel to reach the surface of the water. He dipped his cup into the stream and drank from it, then climbed wheezing back to his feet. The man was in poorer condition than Smith would have guessed and likely had physical difficulties that were not apparent.

"Thank you," Wheeler said. He used a white linen handkerchief to wipe his mouth, then used it also to wipe off the silver cup before he collapsed the article and returned it to his pocket.

Tidy, Smith thought, and meticulous. For a moment Smith was conscious of the contrast between them, Wheeler impeccably dressed and accoutered, Smith ragged and sweaty.

Not that it mattered. Smith waited silently for Wheeler to return to his point.

"I have conferred with my partners in the venture," Wheeler said. "We agree that we can offer you a trespass fee, and mind you this is our final offer, of two thousand dollars cash and one hundred seventy-five dollars per annum thereafter. We feel that the offer is a generous one, Mr. Smith. I hope you will accept it."

"I already told you, it isn't the money. I just don't like that provision about your people controlling the gate. The contract you propose specifically says that you retain the right to lock the gates and control all the keys."

"But surely you understand—"

"Besides, I found Taylor's stakes. He didn't hide them quite well enough."

"There was no intention to hide anything, I assure you. We simply did not want to disrupt the natural beauty of—"

"Those stakes that weren't hidden then, if you insist that they weren't, those stakes that weren't hidden run a long way further than would be necessary for a drinking trough or holding pond, Mr. Wheeler. I could see that much quite plainly. And some of them are paired. Two stakes driven side by side every so often. What do those marks signify, Mr. Wheeler?"

Wheeler smiled and spread his palms. "We, our investors that is, had . . . *considered* . . . the possibility, since the water would be there anyway, we considered that we might someday wish to, well, to add branch canals. To distribute the water over a broader area. You understand." He was still smiling.

"Branch canals," Smith mused. "I think I do understand. I know little about cattle, Mr. Wheeler, but I understand irrigation. You want to irrigate those lower benches for some reason. Hay? Commercial crops? It wouldn't require all that much justification to get a rail spur into the valley, would it? Particularly if some of your investors have any holdings in the railroad. Is that it, Mr. Wheeler?

But what about the people downstream who use that water now? What about them, sir?"

"I've already told you, Mr. Smith. All of the flow will be returned to the original stream bed for downstream use. We already discussed that, if you recall."

"Sure. But there wouldn't *be* any downstream flow. Not enough to count. Not if you used it for bench irrigation, there wouldn't."

"Taylor has figures that I am sure would ease your—"

"I'm sure Mr. Taylor has all manner of figures, Mr. Wheeler. I'm sure he would be glad to show me figures that would prove anything I want them to. Taylor also has some habits that I really don't like, Mr. Wheeler. Like trespassing on my property without my knowledge or permission. Like laying out water systems that I haven't been told about and then hiding the markers from me. That's a form of lying, Wheeler."

Wheeler drew himself up to his full height, a look of indignation coming quick to his freshly shaved cheeks, his jaw set and lips tight. "Regardless of your opinion, sir, I allow *no* dishonor in my business dealings."

Smith gave him a thin smile. "By your lights, Mr. Wheeler, you may even be right about that. But there's a difference between *a* truth and the *whole* truth. Isn't there, Tuck?"

Tuck was taken aback by being suddenly included in the conversation. He looked at Smith and blinked rapidly.

"Never mind," Smith added. "You wouldn't know what we were talking about anyway."

Tuck looked as if he were ready to take quick offense, but Smith was ignoring him and his uncle was paying attention to Smith. Tuck blinked again, shot an ugly glance at Smith and went back to paying attention to the horses he was holding.

"Your rights would be fully protected, Mr. Smith. Contractually protected. I think you must agree that we have been most careful to preserve the integrity of your pond and personal supply of water."

Smith shook his head. "I've been thinking about that ever since I read your contract, Wheeler. The contract is specific about water levels in the pond. It doesn't say anything about outflow from the pond." He waved toward the field of bright green stalks around them. "I depend on the water flow here too, Wheeler. Subsurface irrigation is necessary for my oats to thrive. And I need them for my winter feed. The oats and the hay I cut on the bottom fringes." He shook his head. "I couldn't make it without those, Wheeler. Your contract only guarantees my pond. It doesn't guarantee my livelihood here."

"We have considered, uh, alternatives, Mr. Smith. With exactly that point in mind. It would be much more expensive for us, but we could take our flow downstream from your fields. It would put certain, uh, limitations on our planning. But it could be done. We could draw a new contract. Take our flow from below your field here. I could have the contract available for your signature by tomorrow evening."

Smith looked at the man. A new contract by tomorrow night? That was as good as saying the alternate contract was already drawn and ready for signature. Another thought occurred to him and he asked, "Has the alternate route already been staked and surveyed?"

Wheeler met his eyes. "Yes," he admitted.

"But you would prefer the other," Smith said.

Wheeler shrugged. "The alternate system, because of the loss of elevation, would reduce our irrigation potential by something over three hundred acres. Three hundred fourteen if I remember correctly."

"A minute ago you said you were only 'considering' an irrigation system."

"I don't believe I said 'only.' I did acknowledge that we have been considering such a system. As indeed we have."

Smith grunted skeptically. "The first times we talked it was about water for your cattle to drink."

"But, Mr. Smith, it *is* our intention to provide water for our cattle."

"But that isn't your only intention."

Wheeler spread his hands.

"It makes me wonder, sir, what else you people might be 'considering' that I don't know about."

"I've told you the truth, Mr. Smith."

"If not the whole truth?"

Wheeler shrugged. "One doesn't make one's business plans an open book, Mr. Smith. You understand that, I'm sure."

"Yes," Smith admitted. "I do."

"I hope you will consider—"

Smith shook his head. "I don't think so, Mr. Wheeler." With a quick glance at Tuck he added, "What will you do without my water, Mr. Wheeler?"

Wheeler shrugged again. "We still have stream access for the cattle across the Barber property. We can continue that, uh, phase of our venture here with or without your consent."

Smith nodded. That phase. So the business about the cattle had been wholly a blind. They did not need his water at all for that.

"Think about our offer, Mr. Smith," Wheeler said pleasantly. "I know your position at the moment leans toward refusal, but I do want you to know that the offer remains open. You can change your mind at any time without penalty."

"Thank you, Mr. Wheeler," Smith said solemnly. He had no intention of changing his mind. But by Wheeler's own standard of business ethics, the man was probably being quite generous with him. "If I change my mind I'll let you know."

"Good." Wheeler smiled broadly and held his hand out. Smith shook it without hesitation, and Wheeler made the laborious climb onto the back of the handsome bay horse. Tuck stepped lightly onto his smaller cow pony.

"Good day, sir," Wheeler said pleasantly. He turned the bay back to the creek and splashed across it.

Tuck paused on the near side for a moment to give Smith a dark, hooded look, then wheeled his horse and spurred the animal after his uncle, its hooves throwing a spray of water that was bright and silvery in the afternoon sunlight.

Smith turned back to his work. If they intended to keep the cattle in the valley even without the stream diversion, he still had to get the fencing done.

CHAPTER 22

Smith looked up at the sky and frowned. The sun was slanting well past the usual time, but Susanna still had not shown up for their Sunday-afternoon fishing. He was getting worried about her.

He removed the stem of his pipe from between his teeth and looked down at the rod and fly box by his feet. He could have just gone ahead, of course. He had fished this pond alone or just with the company of a dog for years before the girl had started coming up here. But now it would not seem the same. Instead of the pleasure he usually took in it, the effort would be flat and flavorless. Dammit. Damn that Tuck.

After another minute or two of hesitation, Smith emptied his pipe and jammed it into his pocket, then picked up his things and started down the slope toward the house. His line had never gotten wet.

He put his gear away and stood in the doorway for a moment. Let the team rest, he decided. It was not so far down to the Guynon place. He could walk it.

Smith shoved his hands into his trousers pockets and sauntered off down the path that went by the Guynon place and on into the town.

He wondered if Mrs. Guynon would believe that his visit was a casual thing, that he was merely dropping by on a warm Sunday afternoon.

Probably not, he admitted.

At the very least, then, he hoped she would not object to his call.

He felt a strange tightness in his chest and a faint tickle in his throat. It took him a moment to realize what it was.

Then he laughed aloud at the recognition.

Apprehension.

It had been a *very* long time since anything like that had happened.

This time there was no good reason for it at all.

Feeling wryly amused with himself, Smith walked on at a faster pace.

CHAPTER 23

"Good afternoon, ma'am." Smith removed his hat and held it in front of him.

Before Mrs. Guynon had time to respond there was a loud, glad cry from inside the house, and Susanna came bursting through the door to throw herself in Smith's arms. He smiled and held her, trying to gentle her and ease her sobbing. Her face was red and puffy. It was obvious that she had been crying for some time.

He looked past her to her mother. "She hasn't been like this . . . ever since, uh . . ."

Mrs. Guynon shook her head. "No, thank God. That doesn't seem to have bothered her at all, though how I'll never know. No, she's only been like this this afternoon. Since I told her she couldn't go up to the pond." The woman sighed. "Perhaps I was wrong, Mr. Smith. I don't know. I was just so worried . . ." She let the sentence die.

"I understand." He coughed into his fist and petted the back of Susanna's head again. "I think . . . I really think the fishing is good for her. And she does love it so. Perhaps . . . perhaps in the future . . . you could come with her?"

Mrs. Guynon lowered her eyes, and he hoped it was not his invitation that was making her uncomfortable. "I have so much to do," she said in a small voice. "And I have to take time out for services Sunday mornings." Her eyes raised to his again and she smiled. "That's how Susanna knows it is the day to come to the pond, you know. Every time we go to services she gets excited. I suppose it could be blasphemy to say this, but I think she confuses her visits with you at the pond and her morning visits with the Savior."

"I expect He would understand what's in her heart, Mrs. Guynon, even if we don't understand what is in her head."

"Yes." She smiled again.

Susanna's mother was not unattractive when she smiled, Smith realized. The thought startled him. It was not the sort of thing he generally permitted himself, and he blinked rapidly.

Still, it was the truth. The last time he had seen this woman—really the first time he had ever paid much mind to her—she had been upset and disheveled. Now she was tidy and—he had to think about it for a moment—tidy, in a plain but very quietly pleasant way.

Her gray-streaked brown hair was done up neatly in a tight bun. She wore no powder or tints, of course, but her features were regular and quite nice. She was pale and appeared not to spend much time out-of-doors, but her eyes were large and brown and expressive.

She was wearing a faded and much washed housedress that gave no hint of her figure, but she was nearly as lean as he if not nearly so tall.

All in all a rather nice looking woman without pretensions or artifice.

And, Lord knew, she had a hard enough life trying to keep herself and Susanna. He had no idea how she managed to survive. Certainly there was no opportunity for employment. She likely had to scrape and scrabble for every penny and every scrap of food.

A rush of heat came to Smith's cheeks as he realized the

direction his thoughts were taking him, and he hoped the flush was not visible. To cover it he stammered, "We could make it a real outing for Susanna on her Sundays. You could come with her and watch her fish." He smiled. "She's really learning, you know."

"I know. I can't count the number of times she told me about the trout she caught last Sunday. I don't think I've ever known her to be so excited about anything."

"And after, we could walk down to the house and cook her catch. Right there. We could make a regular party of it." He did not say it but he was thinking that he could certainly spare eggs and cornmeal enough once a week to make sure that Susanna and her mother had a proper feed every Sunday evening. It was something he should have thought of a long time ago.

Except that he had not really known the need. He wondered now if there were other needs unmet that he had been keeping himself too insulated to realize. There was a great deal, obviously, that he failed to know about his neighbors. Yet there he sat, with not a need unmet.

The thought disturbed him.

Mrs. Guynon cocked her head and looked at him as if she were seeing him for the first time. "What about before these outings, Mr. Smith?"

"Ma'am?"

"Susanna and I have never seen you at services, Mr. Smith. Would you go with us?"

Smith blushed. He was sure of it this time. "It's been a long time, Mrs. Guynon."

"All the more reason, Mr. Smith."

"I haven't anything to we—"

"You can wash a shirt, can't you, man?"

"Yes, ma'am."

"Well, then?"

Her jaw was firmly set and her eyes steady—accusingly, he thought—on his. "Well?" she asked again.

"I think . . . perhaps, ma'am. Perhaps I can."

Smith had not thought Susanna was paying any attention to their conversation. She continued to huddle against his chest, allowing him to stroke her although her crying had long since ceased.

With his tentative agreement, though, she began to jump up and down, trying to cling to his arm and to clap her hands at the same time. Her expression was so utterly and openly joyous that an onlooker might have thought she had never had a care in her life.

Smith looked at her and the uncertain set of his mouth softened. He could not deny the child anything that could give her that much pleasure.

"How old is Susanna, ma'am?" he asked abruptly. Even now, looking at her, trying to understand how any man could think of her as a woman, she remained a child.

Mrs. Guynon seemed to understand his question. A look of pain and worry crossed her face. "She's twenty-two, Mr. Smith."

Smith looked at the childlike joy that illuminated Susanna's face from some happy, inner place and shook his head. He persisted in thinking of her as half that age. As perhaps she was.

He glanced toward her mother. Susanna's calendar age probably meant that Mrs. Guynon was in her late thirties, possibly even older than that. It was impossible to tell, really. The life she had led, the gray in her hair and the wrinkles that radiated from her eyes and the corners of her mouth could have been those of a woman anywhere from thirty-five to fifty-five.

Not that it mattered.

Smith smiled at Susanna, and the child hugged him fiercely. *That* was what mattered.

He tugged his right arm free and reached into his coat pocket for the wrap of brown paper he had remembered to bring.

Awkwardly he handed it to Mrs. Guynon. "I thought you might like some juniper bark tea, ma'am."

"You shouldn't have," she said immediately. But there was a bright sparkle of pleasure and interest in her eyes that denied the spoken protest.

"No bother, ma'am. There was some growing where I was cutting wood this week. There isn't anything to it. I, uh, could show you. And Susanna, of course. There's some grows near the pond. Everywhere around here, really."

Mrs. Guynon accepted the fold of wrapped tea from him with a failed effort to hide her eagerness. "Would you show me how to brew it, Mr. Smith? And join us for a cup afterward?"

Smith smiled and nodded. "Yes, ma'am. I'd be pleased to do that."

"Can I build up the fire, Mama? Please?" Susanna broke away from Smith and raced back into the house before her mother had time to answer.

"You be careful now, Susanna. Mind how I taught you." Mrs. Guynon gave Smith a brief smile of apology and hurried inside to keep an eye on Susanna.

Smith thought she had motioned for him to follow, but he was not sure. He hesitated for a moment, wiped his feet carefully and then trailed them reluctantly inside the house. He could not understand why he felt so awkward and unsure of himself this afternoon.

CHAPTER 24

"Oh . . . *hell!*"

Smith dropped the posthole digger and broke into a run, waving his arms and shouting as he raced down toward the oat field.

Cows. Wheeler's damned cows were in his oats. Grazing happily on the young spears of green stalks. Trampling those they did not eat.

The nearest cow—steer it probably really was, although he did not care—raised its head and peered stupidly toward him with sprigs of green oat stem protruding on both sides of its slobbery mouth.

Smith was furious. *And* frustrated.

He shouted again, and the creature spooked, its massive head swinging away from him. Powerful slabs of thick muscle bunched and then sprang into sudden movement as the steer bolted away from him.

The other cattle did not look as if they had seen or heard him, but as soon as the first one moved they were all in motion. They jumped into a panicked run simultaneously, like a single animal, and stormed up the slope away from his oats.

One ungainly, rangy steer with a horn spread of three feet or better brushed clumsily past one of the fenceposts Smith had so laboriously set. The dry aspen post snapped and went flying in a spray of splinters and chunks. The steer seemed not to have noticed.

Smith slowed to a trot and then to a slow, weary walk.

He wanted to . . . do *some*thing. He did not even known what. Shout. Curse. Throw things.

None of that would have had any point whatsoever. The steers certainly would not care. There was no one else around to see or to hear.

Just to vent some of his own anger he bent to pick up a stone and fling it toward the still running, still receding rumps of the cattle. The stone fell a good hundred yards behind the cattle without any of them seeing that he had thrown it. And he did not feel a bit better for the gesture.

Panting, he reached the edge of the oat field and surveyed the damage they had done.

Just how badly the field had been harmed he really could not tell. It might still be early enough in the season for some of the chewed stalks to recover enough to grow and set seed heads. He really was not sure. This was something with which he had never had experience before.

The stalks that had been trampled and torn; he had no idea if they could recover or not.

He did know for sure, though, that he needed this crop. The field of oats represented his entire supply of winter forage and grain, for the horses, for the hens and to a lesser extent for himself. Many of his winter breakfasts, when the pond was iced over and the hens were laying poorly, consisted of hand-milled oats boiled into a porridge or meal. He had tried baking with ground oats, too, using it as a flour substitute, but that had not been so successful.

Regardless, the crop was an important one to him, and its loss would be devastating.

He stood on the edge of the field and glared up both slopes away from the creek bottom.

Some of Wheeler's men should have been in view. He

could nearly always find the horses and then the men whenever he saw the cattle in the distance.

Now he saw nothing. Nothing except the steers.

There were twenty or two dozen of them. They had gotten over their fright already and had come to a stop, spreading out in slow contentment to resume their grazing on the dry grass of the hillsides.

Damn them, Smith muttered to himself. *Damn* them.

He looked at the broken post and the stretch of ground he still had to set posts across before he could even begin to build rails for the fencing.

Damn them.

And the worst of it was that now they had had a taste of the sweet, tender stalks, they would likely be back.

The steers would return in search of more of that good grazing, and likely they would lead others of the herd along with them.

Smith picked up another rock and threw it, feeling the futility of it before he ever bent over but wanting to do it just the same.

Damn them.

There was no help for it, he knew.

He would have to work from sunrise until full dark until the fence was completed and the cattle unable to get to his crop.

In the meantime he would just have to start sleeping down here at the field, catnapping at odd moments when he could and remaining alert through the night to ward off the damned cattle.

He could think of no other way to protect himself for the winter to come.

Damn them.

CHAPTER 25

Smith tried to stifle a yawn, but he just could not do it. He yawned hugely, without feeling the least bit better for it.

He was tired. Lord, he was tired. His eyes felt so gritty and sleep-starved that they actually hurt. It was painful for him to keep them open.

But the damned cattle had not gotten into the oats again. There was that, by golly.

They had tried. Each and every night since that first time they had tried. Drifting back at odd hours of the darkness, lowing and nosing their way through the grass toward the succulent young stalks. Moving along like they had a perfect right to help themselves to his winter forage, damn them.

But they had not succeeded. Every time he had been there to turn them back with shouts and thrown rocks and loud curses, scattering them back into the darkness and away.

He still could not understand how the fool things managed to slip away from the others every night without one of Wheeler's men knowing about it. Or possibly the cowboys only kept the cattle bunched during the day and at night made the mistaken assumption that the herd would stay together. Smith did not know enough about either cowboys or cows to have any valid opinions on that subject. Whatever the reason, every night the stupid beasts had slipped away and tried once again to invade his oat field.

That problem should be ended now though, thank goodness. The fencing was finally done.

Not all of it. The lower, second rails still had to be cut and put in place. But at least there was a solid run of fence around the entire field of oats and around at least a portion of the native grasses, the grass he mowed for wild hay, that grew around the fringes of the oat field. He could take his time about completing the lower string of rails, and in the meantime surely the steers would not try to breach the fence.

He hoped they would not. He needed sleep.

He sighed and looked at the shadows. Susanna and her mother should be coming soon.

If they were coming.

He felt bad about missing the Sunday services he had almost promised to attend with them. There had been no help for it, though. He had had to get those final rails in place. Now he could afford to relax a little. Fish a little. And tonight he could sleep. Inside the house, in his own bed, with Joe on duty outside to attend to the routine of keeping predators away from the hens.

Smith smiled a little. Poor Joe had been confused by his master's change of habits during the past days. Smith had never before slept away from the house, not in the dog's memory anyway, and the experience had seemed a trifle unsettling for the dog.

That was over though, and Smith could explain it to Mrs. Guynon when they got here. Unless she took offense at his failure to go down to town with them this morning and kept Susanna at home again.

Smith turned from the doorway and went back inside

his house to make sure everything was as ready as he could make it.

He had his fishing gear and the bobber-and-line pole he had made for Susanna all ready to go. He had a fire laid and ready to light in the stove. A basket of eggs, many more than they could possibly use, set on the table. Corn-meal batter already prepared and in a bowl.

He might be a sour old bachelor, he thought with some satisfaction, but he could have a meal prepared and be ready for guests as well as anybody. He checked the pot. There was water in it ready for heating and an already measured quantity of freshly ground coffee ready to be put in as soon as the water was boiling. He suspected that Mrs. Guynon would find a taste of coffee to be a real treat. All he had to offer Susanna would be water. Or coffee if she wanted. Had he had the time he could have bought a little milk for her. He had no idea what else to give a child to drink with her meal.

He rubbed his hands fussily together and went from stove to table and back again, satisfying himself again that everything was as ready as he could make it.

Then he turned and went back to the doorway to stand looking downstream. He doubted that Mrs. Guynon would want to come up through the rocks and the trees by the route Susanna usually followed. Probably they would come along the road.

If they came at all. If Mrs. Guynon was not so annoyed with him over his failure to appear for services that she refused to come.

Smith felt a flutter of anxiety such as he had not known since he was a young man. He was so concerned with the possibility that they might not come that he was not even annoyed with himself about it.

CHAPTER 26

Susanna shrieked, and Smith dropped his rod and whirled. Mrs. Guynon jumped to her feet. Both adults were obviously sharing the same thought, the same fear.

The girl squealed again. Her eyes were closed and her jaw set in concentration as she tried to remember the things Smith had so patiently and painstakingly taught her. The tip of her tongue protruded from a corner of her mouth as she tried to restrain her excitement and pull back and up on the pole with one smooth, strong, fluid motion.

The surface of the pond rippled and then erupted as the trout she had successfully hooked whipped its tail from side to side in an effort to flee. Water frothed around it, and Susanna shrieked again.

Smith was nearly limp with relief, but he was grinning broadly as he ran to her to help her beach her fish and remove it from the hook.

"Stillwater. Mama. D'you see? D'you *see?*" She was laughing and grinning and trying to shout all at the same time. Her excitement was contagious, and her mother ran to join them.

Smith carefully held the trout—it was a nice one, ten, perhaps eleven inches long—by a finger hooked through its gill while with his other hand he tried to slip the barbed hook free from its hard, bony lip.

"Hold still. Hold still, honey. I can't get him off the hook if you keep pulling on the line."

Susanna tried with limited success to restrain herself. After a moment she gave it up and dropped the pole onto the ground so she would be free to dance up and down in her pleasure and hug her mother.

"Look here," Smith said proudly. He dropped the line and held the freed fish up at arm's length. Water glistened on its sides in the late-afternoon sunshine, and it wriggled and flopped as it tried still to free itself. "Supper," Smith proclaimed in a loud voice. "And you did it, Susanna. You *did* it. All by yourself."

"Did you see me, Mama? Did you?" She turned to Smith and he held the fish down lower so she could examine it closely. The excitement was still bright in her eyes, and she could scarcely contain herself.

"I saw you, honey," her mother said. She gave Susanna a hug and a kiss on the cheek, and Susanna wriggled with joy.

"I'm so proud of you, Susanna," Smith told her.

She reached out to touch the fish, not trying to take it from him, strangely shy of it now that it was hers. She ran her fingertips over the trout's smooth sides and along the ends of its fins and looked sad as she inspected the tear in its lip where the hook had been set against its struggling.

"You were wonderful, Susanna," Smith said gently. "You did everything *just* right."

Susanna looked at him and grinned.

"You've provided our supper, Susanna," he said.

"You did good, honey," Mrs. Guynon told her with another hug.

Cornmeal, Smith nagged at himself. He had forgotten to put out a shallow pan of cornmeal to roll the fish in. And the skillet of grease they would need to fry them in.

He turned and hurried to fetch the length of twine he used as a stringer so that he could put Susanna's fish onto it and keep it fresh in the pond until they were ready to go down. He was very careful to remember which of the fish on the stringer was hers. He knew it would be special for her to have her very own fish served tonight to her mother and herself.

Smith smiled as he pushed the twine into the gill and out through the trout's mouth. He could not remember when he had spent a more enjoyable afternoon.

CHAPTER 27

Smith pinched the bridge of his nose and laid the book in his lap face down and pages open. He really was going to have to give some thought to the price of spectacles for his reading. He had no idea how much they would cost. Perhaps Ben Frake would already know or could find out. He would have to remember to ask.

He made a mental note too to buy some sweets for next Sunday evening. Horehound candies, possibly. They were not expensive. Smith remembered their flavor from across a good many years. He had always enjoyed them when he was a child. He did not want to do too much, though. If he bought much extra, things an aging bachelor was not likely to keep for himself, Mrs. Guynon was sure to notice. He did not want to insult her with the idea that he was giving charity. This balance between handout and open hand was not something he would have expected to be so complicated. It was not something he had had experience with before.

Smith turned his head as somewhere outside Joe began to growl and snarl with unmistakable fury. He heard the dog's stiff-legged charge at something as he dashed across the gravel, a moment of silence and then a loud flurry of barking as Joe sent something hurrying away in defeat.

Smith gave the dog time to return, then whistled softly.

Joe padded inside, into the lamplight, his tongue out and ruff flat. Whatever it was he had run off, the dog looked pleased with himself.

Smith patted his lap, and the big dog came to drape his forelegs over Smith's thighs and accept the behind-the-ear scratching that was its reward and its pleasure.

He scratched Joe's poll and behind his ears with one hand while the other trailed across his thick, dark fur to find the exquisitely sensitive spot at the base of his tail and scratch there too.

"You're a good old fella, aren't you," Smith said in a soothing voice.

He held the dog's massive head and thought about to-morrow.

Today he had spent around the house, fixing up here and there, mostly using the bow saw to cut green aspen logs into stove-length pieces for faster drying before he split them. That he would do in the early fall after the haying was done.

This evening he felt tired again, his forearms slightly tight and faintly aching from the work with the saw, but it was a good kind of tiredness. It was fine to be back in his bed again after the nights of sleeping outside.

He still had the rest of the rails to put up on the new fenceposts, but there was not so much hurry about that. It could wait another day.

Tomorrow he thought he would drive into town. The egg crate was not quite full but close enough. And he wanted to pick up those things for next Sunday before he turned around and forgot them.

An old joke ran through his memory. Something about memory being the first thing to go when age started to get to a man. And he couldn't remember what the second thing was.

Smith chuckled softly to himself, and Joe rolled his eyes toward Smith's face but was careful not to remove his head from the scratching Smith was absently still delivering.

No, he thought, he did not want to forget those things. And he needed to pick up some more spikes before he could finish the fencing anyway. So he would not really be delaying the job. Not if he looked at it that he needed the spikes before he could finish it.

He wondered if it would be too obvious if he got some tea in addition to his usual coffee order.

Probably, he decided. The juniper tea would do for the time being.

The barbed fishhooks were fine for the moment. Susanna had not lost a single one to a snag yet, and there was certainly nothing in the pond that would break the durable cord he had rigged on her pole.

He smiled to himself as he thought back to the look that had been on the child's face yesterday.

Joe's head and ears came up, and his jaw clamped shut. He pulled away from Smith and slipped out the door again into the night, probably to take a closer look and determine whether he really had heard anything out of place near the coop.

Smith watched the dog until he was out of the dim spread of light that spilled through the open doorway, then picked up his book again. He wiped off a smudge of dirt that Joe had left on the clothbound cover and resumed his reading.

That was another thing he would have to do before summer's end, he reminded himself. Frake should soon have his catalogs together, and Smith would have to make up his list for winter reading.

He grunted, reminding himself to remember the various things tomorrow, then lost himself in the rereading of a favored volume.

CHAPTER 28

Mort Byrnes and his wife were coming out of the store as Smith approached, they and their three children. The kids —the youngest was probably five and the oldest of them not more than eight—were excited. They had candies in their fists, and their cheeks were pouched full like those of chipmunks. The parents were smiling too. Obviously the Byrnes family was having a celebration over something.

The sight of them pleased Smith. It was almost as if he were sharing their happiness, whatever had caused it, and he smiled at them and pulled his hat off in deference to the lady. There was no twinge of jealousy in what he felt when he saw the family, he noticed, and this pleased him too. Once there would have been, however carefully he might have hidden it. He had learned to hide a great many things from other people but never from himself.

He stepped to the side of the plank sidewalk so they could pass.

Byrnes and his wife had been paying attention to something the littlest of their children was trying to tell them. Now they saw Smith, and Byrnes's expression hardened.

Smith gaped in complete disbelief as Mrs. Byrnes—what *was* the woman's name; he could not remember—clucked sharply to her brood like one of his fool hens and actually, *literally,* pulled them into the protection of her skirts.

The littlest of them tried to look around to see what the danger was, but Mrs. Byrnes grabbed the child by the shoulder and turned it so its face was pressed into the blank shield of cloth.

She gave Smith a venomous look, and he could have sworn she came close to hissing at him. Her expression was a mask of utter disgust, and she made no attempt to hide it.

Abruptly she turned, herding her children before her, and swept them down the street in the opposite direction, even though their wagon was parked up the street behind Smith.

One of the children, the middle one, a girl, tried to ask her something, but she hushed it and hurried them all away.

Byrnes lingered behind only for a moment, standing with his head lowered and hooded eyes daring Smith to come closer.

He looked ready to fight, to defend, even though he was a slight man at least half a head shorter than Smith and not so very many years younger.

Smith stared back at him, blinking, totally unprepared for such a reaction as this.

He knew few of the people in the valley, knew none of them really well. But this?

Always he had let them be and asked nothing of them except to be let be in turn. He liked them, as far as that went, including the Byrneses, without feeling close to any of them.

But this?

He could not begin to comprehend what the cause might be. Even as he peered back at a nervous and half-frightened, definitely angry Mort Byrnes he searched his memory for anything, any form of offense or unseemly conduct, that might justify this reaction on their part.

There was nothing. Nothing that he could think of.

He blinked again, and Byrnes turned away with a low, huffy snort and hurried up the street to join his family, trailing a pace or two behind them, again as if protecting them, and glancing back over his shoulder now and then toward the immobile, bewildered Smith.

Smith watched them out of sight as the whole family scurried into Isom Wilson's harness shop, then shook his shoulders to throw off a chill. He shuddered once and slowly, wonderingly, made his way blindly into Frake's store.

"I will not be needing your produce again, Mr. Smith," Ben Frake said with stiff formality. His mouth worked around the syllables as if each word had the taste of bile, and his shoulders were rigidly set.

Smith had a definite impression that the speech was one Frake had practiced and refined long before Smith's appearance in the store today. And in anticipation of it.

"I have your account prepared," Frake said. His voice was almost toneless.

The storekeeper turned and picked up a sheet of paper and the handful of coins that had been piled atop it on a small shelf behind his counter.

Automatically Smith accepted both the paper and the money. He glanced down at the sheet. It was half filled with tight, crabbed handwriting and figures.

The final entry, he noted, charged him for a dozen barbed fishhooks. The same ones that Frake had said would be his gift to Susanna.

Smith looked up and met Frake's eyes. The storekeeper's look wavered only for an instant, then steadied, his lids drawing close and tight with determination.

Whatever this was about, it had been thoroughly pondered and then firmly decided.

There was no apology in Frake's look. They were alone in the store. The man could have said something to soften this blow if he had wished, and no one would have been the wiser about it.

This was something *he* wanted to do.

Smith belatedly realized that Frake had called him *Mr.* Smith. That was something the man had not done in years.

Smith still did not understand. He could not begin to imagine what had caused this change.

He parted his lips, wanting to speak, wanting to ask why.

Pride would not allow it.

His jaw took on a hard set, and his lips pulled together in a thin, tight line.

He nodded abruptly and shoved the coins into his pocket uncounted. It would have been pointless to count them anyway. After all these years the storekeeper could well have decided to add to Smith's "punishment" by cheating on the ledger entries. Smith would not have known.

And at the moment Smith would not have cared.

Silent, still in confusion but absolutely refusing to let any of that show, Smith turned and marched with a stiff, even gait out of Ben Frake's store.

The hell with them. One and all.

CHAPTER 29

The eggs were still in their crate, still in the back of the wagon. There was no market for them now, it seemed. And no point in brooding about that. What was done could not be changed. The fact that he had no idea what it was that *had* been done did not matter either.

Smith frowned. There was no other market for his surplus. Certainly none within the valley. Not unless individuals wanted to buy from him. And judging by the reactions of the Byrnes family, that would be most unlikely.

Beyond the valley there would certainly be outlets for anything he might produce. But he had no way to transport anything as fragile and as perishable as eggs.

He frowned again, trying to work out an alternative to the system of exchange that had sustained him for years. He could think of nothing.

On the other hand, he realized, he had been here before there had ever been a store in the valley. Before there had been any other permanent residents here.

He expected to still be here when the others had given up and gone or until he died. Whichever came first.

He would get along.

He glanced over his shoulder toward the crate that was jostling from side to side with the movement of the wagon wheels over the bumps and ruts of the trace that passed for a road.

If he took them home with him they would only spoil.

There was no way he could possibly use all of the egg production himself. He had expanded his laying flock by way of the spring setting clutches to meet the market Ben Frake had provided. Now it seemed that he was left with too many hens and far too many eggs.

He laughed aloud as the solution to that problem came to him. The laugh came out as a short, bitter bark of sound, but it was a laugh nonetheless.

When he reached the turnoff to the Guynon place downstream from his he turned into it, although he almost had to argue the point with Jake. The horse knew good and well where they were supposed to go once they left the store. Or thought he did.

Explanations would be in order when he got there, Smith decided as he drove. But not too much. He would want to convince Mrs. Guynon that this was surplus and not a handout. All of the specifics should not be necessary.

Smith snorted softly to himself. Not that he knew them all himself anyway. Still there was no point in weeping to strangers.

He smiled a little and spoke gently to the team. Something good could come of almost anything. At least this would be of benefit to the girl and her mother. There was something to be said for that, after all.

CHAPTER 30

"No!" Smith began to run, shouting and waving his arms.

It was not yet dawn. The dim, watery light of the false predawn gave the only visibility, and the air was chilling. He had been on his way to the backhouse before getting ready to chore.

Now in the thin, faint light he could see dark shapes moving below him along the creek. Moving *in the oat field.*

Barefoot and wearing only his long johns he ran down to the edge of the field, ducked under the single rail on that side of the field and charged the cattle with loud roars.

The steers snorted and whirled, racing back the way they had come.

Miraculously they managed to thunder through the two-rail gap in the fence without shattering any posts or knocking down any more of the laboriously emplaced rails.

Smith came to a panting halt, anger catching at his lungs every bit as much as the brief spurt of exertion.

Damned beasts, he muttered to himself, as he bent forward trying to catch his breath.

Belatedly Joe loped to his side to sit by his foot with his tongue hanging out. Cattle and crops were not his concern. Predators and hens were.

Smith gave the dog a quick, undeserved scratch behind the ears and then picked his way through the oats to the broken fence.

The single rail had not been enough to keep the steers out. He was going to have to get the second rank of rails cut and erected as quickly as possible.

He tried to assess the damage that had been done to the crop by this latest intrusion, but it was still too dark. With any degree of luck it would not be too bad. The steers had still been drifting into the field when he saw them, although probably they had had time to pause on the edge near the fence and graze there for a while before they moved deeper into the young growth.

As he reached the fence, though, and examined the downed rails his jaw firmed, and a flush of hot, quick anger washed through him.

The cattle had not broken down the single rails. The aspen saplings had been pulled away from the posts and thrown upslope. Discarded there.

If the steers had pushed their way through, the down rails should likely have been broken and certainly would have been carried inside the field from the press and the push of the hungry cattle.

Instead they lay uphill, outside the line of posts, very obviously pulled free and discarded there.

The light was poor, but he examined the rails with his fingertips as well as by sight. He was sure that at one end of each he could feel abrasions in the bark where ropes had gouged and worn.

Smith began to tremble from the emotions that were boiling within him, but none of it showed in his expression or action.

Very calmly he walked upslope away from the fence and felt of the ground surface with his bare soles. He searched thirty feet or so out from the fence and quickly found what he expected there. Gouges in the soil surface where a horse, quite certainly with a rope on its saddle horn, had dug in to pull.

Someone . . .

He could not imagine who or why. More accurately, he could not decide among the several possibilities. The assault—which was what he clearly considered it to be—could have been Asa Wheeler's doing. It could as easily have something to do with whatever trouble there had been in town that made Ben Frake and the Byrnes family react as they had. He still did not know what that was all about, but he had seen unreasoning hatreds before. This could be another, similar outbreak of irrational ugliness.

A chill rode his spine, and he was not naïve enough to think it had anything to do with the cold morning air.

Calmly, with slow deliberation, he picked up the discarded rails and carried them back to the fence line. They would go back in place and the second line as well, and if necessary he would move his bed down here to the field until harvest.

Whoever, whatever, this problem was all about, he was not leaving.

Not this time.

CHAPTER 31

Smith smiled. With a flourish he clicked his heels together, bowed gracefully and whisked the platter down onto the tabletop. "For you, ma'am," he proclaimed.

Susanna squealed and clapped her hands excitedly. Half of the platter was occupied with two fish. Two fish she had caught herself, then allowed Smith to clean for her. Now they were her supper, split, rolled in cornmeal and fried to crisp perfection. One of the two was of quite a nice size. The girl did not seem to mind in the least that the other was tiny, barely large enough to provide a mouthful of white, flaky meat. She was as proud of one as of the other, and Smith had taken just as much trouble to ensure the perfection of the one as of the other. Her face creased wide with her grin, and she laughed happily.

Smith winked at Mrs. Guynon and turned to get the rest of the meal from the stove. In addition to more fish there was corn bread—light and moist and slightly sweet, just the way he liked it best—and eggs. They had eggs enough to feed a platoon, he reflected. Susanna loved eggs, though. The platter he had set before her was heaped with eggs fried so the whites were firm but the yolks a soft, golden fluid. He poured coffee for himself and Mrs. Guynon and gave Susanna a glass of water. He had not gotten the milk for her, and now it looked as if he would have to send out-of-valley for it if he intended to.

Was it possible to buy evaporated milk by mail order?

He was not sure. He was going to have to send off for catalogs. He knew that. And he was entitled to use of the mails. No one could halt that, no matter what they thought.

Milk if he could then and possibly coffee. Although he could get along without coffee if he had to. It was really a luxury. He had been without it when he first came here, when he was the only resident.

It was amazing, he realized, how soft and dependent he had become in these past few years. How much he had come to take things for granted.

But he had been without before. He could learn to do it again.

Besides, with no produce to sell he was going to have to cut back anyway. Coffee would be a very good place to start.

He smiled to himself as he pulled out his chair and took his seat between Mrs. Guynon and Susanna. Perhaps next Sunday they should vary the menu and include fried chicken on the platters.

He started to reach automatically for the serving spoon, then snatched his hand back away from it and ducked his head as he recognized and too late remembered the silent prayer Mrs. Guynon and Susanna engaged in before each meal. That was a habit he had long been away from, and it was difficult to remember now.

"Amen," Mrs. Guynon said aloud.

"Amen," Susanna echoed.

The girl dug at her trout with a fork and grinned at Smith. "These're my very own, aren't they, Stillwater?"

"They surely are, honey. Your very own."

She took a mouthful and chewed it slowly, pretending a

thoughtful expression. "I think they're the best ol' trout I ever tasted, Stillwater."

He smiled at Susanna and passed her mother the heavy platter of fried eggs.

CHAPTER 32

"You son of a bitch."

Smith lowered the hand he had just raised in greeting and stared at the man. He recognized him, of course. It was Russell, Barber's neighbor from far downvalley. His two sons were with him in the wagon. They had axes and saws with them but did not look as if they had been doing any woodcutting.

Smith laid his own saw carefully aside. "What was that?"

"You heard me," Russell said.

"Yes, I believe I did," Smith said calmly.

"This wood's for honest men," Russell said. "You stay the hell away from it."

"I've never seen you cutting up this high," Smith said, still calm. "Did you come here for wood or to pick a fight?" He stepped over the trunk of the aspen he had just felled and faced the man.

Russell wrapped the lines of his team around his whip socket and jumped down to the ground. His boys joined him. The boys were probably sixteen and eighteen and big enough to do men's work. They stood flanking their father with their fists balled and anger flushing their cheeks.

"I see," Smith said softly.

"This is our grove," Russell said. "You stay out of it."

Smith looked at the man and then at each of his boys. The boys were young. There was a great deal they would not know. And Russell. Tod Russell was not nearly as hard a man as he believed himself to be.

Smith felt the old, familiar churning in his stomach. The knotting. The anger. The tightening of his flesh around his eyes. The rising, sweeping, overwhelming surge. His hands knotted into fists, and he began to shake.

No.

Abruptly he turned away from them. He had done nothing, absolutely nothing, to cause it but all of a sudden he was breathing heavily, the air rasping in and out of hard-pumping lungs.

No!

He sought to control it. To control himself. There was nothing he could do about them. They were fools anyway, he told himself.

He bent down and very carefully picked up his saw and carried it to the wagon, laid it gently into the bed.

His morning's work lay scattered on the ground around him, half a load of trimmed saplings for rails and half a load of full logs that still had to be cut into manageable lengths before one man could load them.

He was shaking and moved with a slow and careful deliberation as one item by another he began to gather up his tools and place them in the bed of the wagon.

The horses were picketed down on the grass below the trees. They ignored him, not expecting to be put back into the traces until late afternoon.

"Don't turn your back on me, you son of a bitch," Russell barked.

"Don't you insult *us,*" one of the boys added. Smith did not look to see which of them had spoken.

He heard the thud of boot soles on soil and tensed, unable to stop himself from that but unwilling to turn to face them.

His fists clenched again involuntarily, and the muscles at his neck corded. His breathing was coming faster again. But he had control now. He would not lose that. He refused to. He would *not*.

He stood, braced, and one of them slammed into the backs of his legs just above the knees, driving him forward and down with his knees grinding into the gravel. The cloth of his trousers shredded, and he could feel the bits of sharp stone cut into his flesh.

He tried to concentrate on that and willed himself to remain still.

A second one piled onto his back, exploding the air from his lungs and sending him face forward onto the ground. Grass and dead leaves tickled his face, and the smell of dust and sun-warmed earth was strong and dry in his nostrils.

He tried to concentrate on the various delicate scents that made up the overall odor of soil and was only faintly aware of the dull, deep impact of a boot toe driving into his side and another that tore at his buttocks.

There were three of them, but they did not know what they were doing and they got in each other's way.

They kicked and pummeled and swore, and Smith curled himself into a tight ball and covered his temples with his arms to keep them from doing real damage.

"Cowardly son of a bitch," one of the boys rasped. He sounded close to exhaustion.

"We knew that," Russell said.

One of them kicked Smith in the meat of the thigh and another dropped onto his back and began to punch the back of his head.

They were not very good, Smith reflected dreamily, but there seemed to be a great many of them.

He was aware that his thoughts were misting and beginning to swim. He supposed he should be concerned about that, but at the moment he was not. There would be time enough for that later.

They continued to kick him. He knew they were doing it, but he did not particularly mind at the moment. He could hear the impacts more than he could feel them, and it all seemed quite far away.

They cursed some more, the boys echoing their father's language, and kicked and hit some more. But they were all growing tired now. The blows did not seem very painful. He could hear their breathing, and it was as ragged as his own.

After a little while Smith went away from them, although he was not sure quite how he had done that. He could not remember moving or going anywhere, but the Russells and their grunting and cursing and kicking faded until Smith felt himself floating comfortably free of them.

It was pleasant where he was then. Warm. And he was not eager to go back.

He thought he could hear himself snoring, and he found that interesting in a detached and distant sort of way. He did not think he had ever heard himself snore before.

When he woke he wished immediately that he could go back again to the cloud-soft comfort. The pain was like a tangible wall of fire and coals that he had to crawl through on hands and knees. He could not see well, and it took him several minutes of intense concentration to decide that he could not see because it was late, dusk, and there was little light.

He moved, straightening his body, and cried out aloud at the pain that knotted his stomach and legs and lower back. One of the horses whickered an answer, a low, rumbling complaint because the evening unharnessing and feeding was overdue, and Smith groaned. The horses still had to be hitched, and home was more than a mile away. He did not know how he was going to do what had to be done, but there was no one else to do it.

Eyes shut and face filmed with greasy sweat, he drew in shallow breaths to fill his lungs and gathered his resolve, then crawled slowly up until he could lurch to his feet.

He swayed and tottered. But he was upright. He blinked. The horses were there, where he had left them. The wagon was behind him, uphill.

There was no sign of the Russells.

Grimly, very careful of the placement of each foot, wincing at the movement of each and every separate muscle, he began the slow and painful journey down to Jack and Jake.

It could have been worse, he kept telling himself, but somehow that gave him scant comfort.

CHAPTER 33

The pain had gotten worse, not better. He tried to sit up, and the pain wrenched at his gut and coursed through him like fire. Sweat broke out on his forehead again, and he vomited on the floor beside his bed.

He felt ashamed. The shame of it was worse than the pain or the stench, but there was nothing he could do about it. He lay back on the bed, weak and limp, and was shamed further because his hens and the stout, patient horses needed tending and he could not get to them to care for them. They were his responsibility, and he was letting them down.

He tried again to rise, but he could not do it. This time when he lay back on the sweat-soaked blanket it was all he could do to keep from crying.

The doorway and window were in shadow, but he did not know whether it was morning or evening. He tried but could not so much as remember whether a full day had passed. He had been unconscious. Now he felt himself drifting again.

At least this time it felt like a healing sleep instead of passing out when he slid into the relief of it.

For some time—he had no idea how long it was—he slipped in and out of a hazy, half-aware state. Conscious and not at one and the same time.

It was eerie yet at the same time comforting. When he had time and ability to reflect on it he likely would find it interesting. Until then he was only able to make note of it and try to absorb the sensations. Concentrating on that was much better than thinking about his situation or about the animals that still had to be tended.

He dreamed part of the time, the dreams mingling with memory, intertwining until he could not be sure what was dream and what was memory.

Part of the memory he did not want to separate from the dreaming.

Part of it was easier to accept as dream than as memory.

He moaned and cried out, tried to sit up and was driven back onto the bed by the fierce onslaught of pain.

He shuddered and ground his teeth together.

Smell. Can you dream an odor? Or must that be memory? He was not sure he wanted an answer.

The smells were there, though. He could almost have sworn they were there.

Smoke. Woodsmoke and the smoke of burned gunpowder. Beneath those the smells of unwashed bodies and long-unwashed clothing. Smoke and blood and, cutting through it all, underlying the other odors, a sharp, sickening, sweetish stink of decomposure. Decomposing flesh. Manflesh. Rotting. Rotten.

He screamed and found himself bolt upright on the smelly bed with new sweat cold on his face and the lingering echo of his scream hanging in his ears. He was so startled that he welcomed the pain the motion had caused him. It at least gave him a point of contact with reality. He wanted to get up now, to get about his chores, but the pain shifted from asset to enemy and forced him down onto the bed again, writhing and groaning.

Sound.

He winced and shivered as he dreamed/remembered the sounds.

Rattle after long, rattling roll of sounds. Dull, distant, brittle reports. Nearer, louder, booming explosions. Metal clanging brightly against metal. The creak of leather and the plod of footsteps.

Footsteps. Slow and weary. Quick and frantic.

Men running. Men screaming. Horses neighing in terror and in pain. Men crying.

And a low, subdued, ugly tearing sound that he knew he should recognize but did not. Dared not.

His eyes flew open, and he held himself rigid. Not against the pain. Against the memory. Pain now would be a welcome distraction. It was the sound that he feared. The ugly, awful sound that he dared not remember or he would go utterly mad. He knew he would, and he was afraid.

Somehow, not even trying now to fight the pain, he forced himself off the bed and onto his feet. He staggered out into the yard, gulping at the fresh, untainted air and clutching both arms over his belly as if to hold himself together.

He tottered, frantic with worry, glad of the relief the overwhelming pain gave him, to the chicken coop and the grain barrel.

Carrying water to them would be the worst of it. He would manage it. Somehow.

The horses he would just turn loose to graze along the creek. They would not go far.

Joe nosed at his leg and licked Smith's hands. Smith wished he could sit down in the filth of the chicken yard and wrap his arms around the dog's neck and cry into his ruff. But he could not. If he went down he might not be able to get up again.

And if he rested now, he might remember.

The thought of that terrified him, and he shoved the dog

rudely away and bent to reach for the water bucket. The pain knotted and churned inside him, and he was glad of it.

He thought of going back to the bunk, sleeping, dreaming, remembering, and he began to shudder and sob.

The movement and the pain were far better alternatives than that.

His cheeks were tracked with moisture, although he had not thought he was sweating so much now. He wiped them with the back of his wrist and tasted salt where some of the fluid was smeared over his lip. He could not understand that.

He let himself out of the chicken pen and went to the horse trough to dip out some water. It was closer than the creek, and he would not have to bend so low.

When he tried to pick the bucket up he felt as if something tore across the lower part of his stomach, and he was wrapped in a flood of gray.

He felt the loss of balance, felt himself begin to fall. By the time he hit the ground he could feel nothing.

There was no sensation at all.

Blessedly, there were no dreams nor memories either.

There was nothing.

CHAPTER 34

He gagged and tried to cough. Something was wrong. He not only thought he could smell strange smells, he thought he could even taste strange and wonderful flavors. It was neither dream nor memory. He was sure of that. He just could not identify what this was.

Smith opened his eyes. It took him a moment to focus, and he had difficulty getting the left eye open. It was glued shut from mucus.

A cool, damp cloth helped him get it open, and he could see Mrs. Guynon bending close above him. Susanna was behind her mother with a pail in her hand. The child had been crying. Her face was flushed and mottled and her eyes red-rimmed and swollen.

Smith felt the heat of acute embarrassment in his cheeks. He was inside the house, on his own bed. The last he remembered he had been out in the yard. By the trough, he thought. He was not sure about that.

His nose told him that Susanna and her mother must have been here for some time. They had obviously cleaned up his mess. That made his embarrassment all the deeper.

"Lie still, Mr. Smith." Mrs. Guynon passed the deliciously cool cloth over his forehead and face again, and Susanna put the pail down and knelt beside him.

The child kissed his temple wetly and began to cry again.

He tried to speak, but a croak was all he could get out.

He struggled, trying to sit up. He realized that he had no idea what, if anything, he was wearing, and he worried about that too.

"Susanna." Mrs. Guynon spoke sharply. "Did you forget what I asked you to do?"

"But, Mama—"

"Mr. Smith is going to be all right, Susanna. You want to help don't you?"

Susanna nodded, her face twisted in an agony of fretfulness.

"Then do what I asked you, dear."

Reluctantly she nodded again, gave Smith another worried look and went to pour water from the pail into the big pan Smith used for heating his dishwater.

"I couldn't find your laundry tub, Mr. Smith," Mrs. Guynon said. "Do you have one?"

Smith shook his head. The movement was painful but nothing he could not stand. The pains in his back and belly and legs were still there, but they were duller now, more bearable.

He tried to speak to her, to explain, but again he had difficulty forming words. He wondered how long he had been like this. And how long Mrs. Guynon and Susanna had had to be here.

"In a moment, Mr. Smith. Take some of this first." She knelt beside the bed and picked up a bowl that must have been out of sight on the floor.

The smell of it was what had brought him awake. She must have trickled some into his mouth also, because there was a lingering taste in his mouth. It was similar to but not exactly like something he very dimly remembered from a very long time ago. He questioned her with his eyes.

"Chicken broth, Mr. Smith. Very rich. I added extra fat.

And I drizzled some beaten egg into it as well. Do you think you could take some now?"

He nodded.

She had to spoon it to his mouth. He found that he had strength enough to raise his arm only a matter of inches. Even that little bit was enough to leave him shaken and weak. He could not possibly have held the spoon for himself.

"There." She pushed the spoon between his parted lips and tilted it.

The warm, yellow, slightly salty liquid flowed soothingly through his throat and spread a small glow of warmth in his stomach. He doubted that he had ever tasted anything quite so wonderful.

"Thank you." He got the words out this time and tried to let his head fall back onto the bed, but she propped him up and dipped the spoon into the bowl again with a smile.

"You have a long way to go, Mr. Smith. Don't go back to sleep on me now."

"How—" He grimaced. "How long?"

"How long were you out? I'm sure I don't know. You were outside on the ground when we found you." She smiled. "Thank the good Lord your dog knew Susanna. He wouldn't allow me anywhere near you. That was yesterday afternoon. It is midafternoon Monday now. Does that answer some of your questions?"

He nodded weakly and accepted another sip of the wonderful broth.

Monday. They had found him Sunday. He tried to remember what day of the week it had been that he went up to cut wood, but he could not. He was still muzzy and confused about a great many things. That was only a very minor point among them.

It even took him a moment to remember who had done

this to him and how it had happened. He could remember clearly enough, though, that he had had no idea at the time why. He still did not.

He rolled his head to the side and could see a pallet of folded blankets laid out on the floor on the far side of the house. It was wide enough for two and apparently Mrs. Guynon and Susanna had been sleeping there.

"I'm sorry . . . you've had to—"

"Tush, Mr. Smith. And please be quiet. We've done nothing that any decent person would not do, and we'll have no more talk about that, sir."

"But—"

"Hush." He wanted to say more, to protest that she had done more than was necessary already, but she stopped him by pouring another spoonful of broth into his mouth. He could either close his mouth and swallow it or drool it all over himself. He stopped trying to speak and swallowed.

He swallowed quickly and tried to speak.

"I know, Mr. Smith. I know exactly what you are trying to tell me, but we are staying. Why, I couldn't drag Susanna home now if I wanted to. Which I certainly do not. So save your protests, sir. It is no inconvenience to us, Lord knows. We haven't any livestock to watch over. Just our garden, and that does not require much care." She smiled again. "Besides, Susanna is *so* proud of being able to feed your chickens. I showed her how. I hope you don't mind."

"Mind?" Smith groaned and closed his eyes for a moment. When he opened them again Mrs. Guynon looked worried, and he smiled to assure her. "I can't begin to . . . tell you, ma'am—"

"I understand. You don't have to say more."

"But please, ma'am. I can . . . I can sleep out in the barn. It wouldn't be right—"

"Hush." She reinforced it by shoving another spoonful of the soup into him.

Smith wanted to say more, to explain, to protest. But his stomach was positively radiating warmth from the broth, and his eyes were being pulled closed by a very insistent sleepy lassitude.

Later, he thought. They could discuss it later. As soon as he rested. Just for a moment.

CHAPTER 35

They stayed another two days, keeping him closely confined to his bed and, by Wednesday afternoon, to a pillowed chair at the table, before he could convince them that he was capable of managing for himself.

The truth was that his ability to manage remained in doubt, but he was in a constant state of embarrassment while the two females were present. He found it a great relief when they finally agreed to go home.

"We'll be back tomorrow evening to fix your dinner and clean up, Mr. Smith," Mrs. Guynon warned. "And don't you do a thing about the washing. Remember, you promised."

"Yes, ma'am," Smith lied solemnly. "I'll remember."

Mrs. Guynon gave him a soft-eyed look and seemed to want to say more, but she did not. She nodded and turned away to pick up the small bundle of things she had brought to the house over the past few days.

Susanna looked as if she might cry. She gave Smith a hug, which hurt his still aching ribs, and kissed him on the neck, then followed her mother out to the path toward town.

Smith felt bad that he could not drive them home, but he knew they would refuse the offer. Besides, he was not entirely sure he would be able to lift the sets of harness onto Jack and Jake quite yet.

Instead he had to settle for standing in the doorway and

watching them out of sight. Joe padded to his side and sat with his rump warm on Smith's shoe and his back pressed tight against Smith's leg to accept a scratching. The dog had been unusually attentive the past few days, hanging close to the house during the day and only leaving Smith's side at night to take up his guard duties.

Smith sighed and went back to pour himself a cup of the juniper tea Mrs. Guynon had made and left for him. He was moving much more easily now, but some support would be welcome. He did not own a cane, had never had need of one, but tomorrow, he decided, he would see what he could find that might serve as a staff he could lean on. He was actually looking forward to being able to do his own chores in the morning.

Smith groaned and leaned against the hoe he was using as a walking stick.

"Bastards," he muttered aloud. Joe tilted his head to the side and gave Smith a questioning look. The word was not any command he was familiar with.

Smith stood behind the house, surveying the damage he could see and trying to guess at what he could not see from here.

Sometime while he had been laid up, someone had come back to pull more fence rails down. Two of the posts had been roped and dragged down as well. Cattle had been grazing freely on the young oat crop, drawn to the succulent shoots over and over again in preference to the hard, dry grasses of the hillsides.

Smith made his way slowly down to the field and ducked under the rails that had been left standing on the near side of the fence line. He was pleased to discover that he was moving with some degree of comfort now. But that was about all that pleased him at the moment.

The bright green carpet of oats should have been a uniform twelve to fourteen inches high now. Instead it was ragged and patchy, chewed almost to ground level in some places, virtually untouched in others.

There was still time for some recovery, he thought. Hoped. But it was certain that his yield would not be anything close to what it should have been and would have been had the steers not been turned onto it.

A bark of sharp, bitter laughter erupted from him. This winter he wouldn't need so much grain anyway. With no market for the eggs he had been producing he had no reason to carry so many hens through the winter.

Fried chicken. Roast chicken. Boiled chicken. Chicken soups. Chicken broth. Chicken and dumplings. Much of his winter eating was up in the coop right now busily producing useless eggs.

He would have to send out for some water glass to pack eggs in for future use. They would keep for months in a crock, immersed in water glass.

And he really should get some pickling salts too, he thought. He could hard-boil eggs, peel them and pickle them by the barrelful.

Come to think of it, he realized, there just might be a market for pickled eggs even if he could not transport them fresh. It would be worth looking into.

He leaned on the hoe handle and moved across to the other side of the field, uncaring now about where he placed his feet among—or directly on—the plants.

There was still the fence to repair so he could salvage as much as possible from this intrusion.

The aches and deep pains did not permit him to look forward to that work, but it was something that had to be done. It was time he got to it.

CHAPTER 36

"Asa wants to see you," Tuck said. He managed to make the simple message sound insolent. He sat on his horse, a much better quality mount than Smith had seen him ride before, with an arrogant cockiness that rubbed Smith the wrong way.

"I'll be at home if he wants me. Almost anytime." Smith moved idly toward the side of Tuck's horse, leaning on the hoe more than was really necessary. He was feeling considerably better now. Almost normal.

"An important man like Asa, Mr. Smith, I figure you should go to him." Tuck grinned nastily. "An' I want to be there to watch you do your begging."

Smith looked up at him with genuine amusement. Beg? Tuck seemed to actually believe it.

"Why didn't Charlie bring the message himself?" he asked casually as he stopped at the off side of Tuck's saddle. He had to tilt his head far back to look the young idiot in the eyes.

"Devore?" Tuck laughed. "He ain't with the outfit anymore. Him and Asa got into a disagreement over something. I wouldn't know what, of course." He was still smirking.

"No, I'm sure you wouldn't."

"Asa made me foreman once Devore quit. So any messages. Or whatever." He grinned. "I'll be in charge."

"Yes, I'm sure you will," Smith said softly. He reached

out and fingered Tuck's lariat. The hemp rope was coiled and hung beside Tuck's saddle horn. Smith felt of the hondo and ran his fingertips along the inside of the rope at the loop end.

A flicker of annoyance crossed Tuck's face, and he booted his horse sharply in the side to move it away from Smith. "What the hell d'you think you're doing?"

Smith gave him a look of innocent surprise. "Why, looking for splinters. Bits of bark. You know."

Tuck scowled for an instant, then relaxed. "You wouldn't have the guts to do anything if you did find what you're looking for, Smith. We both know that, don't we?" He laughed.

"What— Oh, of course. You mean because I didn't turn you in for rape."

Tuck laughed again. "It wasn't that nohow, Smith. She was willing enough. I could swear to that in a court of law."

"I'm sure you would," Smith agreed.

"Sure. I gave her a pretty, an' she said okay. Nothing wrong with that now, is there. Any judge would tell you so. No need for swearing anyhow. You sure ain't gonna tell anyone. You likely know what I'd do to you if you said anything about it." He snorted. "I hear you already got a taste of what you could expect if you tried to cross me." Tuck seemed to be enjoying himself.

Smith looked at him with a certain amount of disbelief. The fool seemed to actually believe that it had been the threat of his retaliation and not Susanna's welfare that had kept Smith quiet about it. He wondered how Tuck might have rationalized Mrs. Guynon's silence.

There was no telling, Smith realized. The boy would have been able to convince himself of anything.

Smith considered for a moment explaining to Tuck just

why he and Susanna's mother had remained silent. But there would have been no point to it. Tuck would not have believed him anyway. If by some miracle Tuck believed, he still would not be able to understand. No, Smith thought, there was no point in explanations.

As for Tuck believing Smith to be a coward, there was no point in discussing that either. The boy would never be able to comprehend that, nor did Smith feel inclined to explain himself to the likes of this cowboy. He could just go on believing whatever he wished. Smith had had worse thought of him and by better men than John Friar would ever be.

Smith turned away and began to limp back toward the house, leaning heavily on the hoe handle.

"Don't turn your back on me, you son of a bitch," Tuck snapped.

Smith did not bother to look at him again. He heard the creak of leather as Tuck stepped down to the ground and started toward him.

"I told you that Asa wants—"

There was a low growl of warning from over by the barn, and Joe came into view at a run with his tail held stiff and his hackles raised. His teeth gleamed yellow-white, and there was no question that he meant business.

Tuck yelped once and turned back for his horse and the safety of the saddle.

He hit the saddle in a leap and yanked at the butt of a carbine he carried in a leather boot at the side of the saddle.

"Joe!" Smith said sharply, and the dog skidded to a stiff-legged halt.

The horse was nervous, shifting and pawing on the edge of control. Tuck fumbled the carbine out of its scabbard. It was a model Smith had seen before but was not familiar with. Tuck worked a lever beneath the action and swung the muzzle toward the dog.

Smith snapped his fingers and pointed to a spot on the ground behind him. Obediently Joe came to him and sat where Smith indicated.

"I could shoot you too, Smith," Tuck hissed. His face was still pale from his fright.

Smith nodded. "You'd have to," he said calmly.

Tuck looked at Smith and then at the dog behind him on the ground. He licked his lips nervously. Smith did not move. The hoe in his hand, the closest thing he had to a weapon, remained on the ground.

"Just you remember to keep your mouth shut," Tuck warned. "Or you know what I'll do to you. An' you'd better get a move on. Asa's expecting you."

"Wheeler knows where to find me."

"I told you—"

Smith turned his back on Tuck, snapped his fingers and went back inside the house with Joe close at his heels. After a long, silent minute he heard a curse from the yard and then the sound of Tuck's horse thundering out of the yard at a sudden run.

Smith felt himself begin to shake, and sweat appeared on his forehead.

He was beginning to have doubts. He did not know if he could do it any longer.

He wanted to get down on his knees and pray.

But he had abrogated that right a long time ago.

Instead he sat, suddenly weary, and petted Joe's massive head.

CHAPTER 37

Smith slid half a dozen fried eggs off the platter to the plate that had been set in front of him and smiled as Susanna proudly and with great care, the tip of her tongue protruding slightly from the corner of her mouth, filled his cup with juniper tea.

There was no longer any real need for Mrs. Guynon and Susanna to make the walk up from their home to cook for him. He was feeling quite well enough to handle his own needs again. But it had become virtually a habit now for all three of them; it let him know for certain that they were eating well. And, in truth, he had come to rather enjoy their company.

Still, they should not have to make the walk each and every evening. It would be better if he took his day's gather of eggs and a little of this or that and drove down to their home for the occasional meal. It was something they could discuss shortly.

He took a very small portion of the corn bread Mrs. Guynon had baked and waited for the women to join him at the table and say their blessing.

He wondered if there might be some tactful way he could show Mrs. Guynon how to make corn bread. She was an excellent cook. Really she was, he assured himself. She made the eggs much more flavorful than he ever could, and she was adept at using spices and condiments that he had impulsively collected over the years but rarely if ever actually used.

But her corn bread. He restrained himself from the headshake he almost forgot and displayed. Smith had to confess that he liked his own far better.

She was kind enough to make it, though, so he could darn well eat it. He smiled at her, nodded and took another small piece.

"You've gotten a lot done, Mr. Smith."

"Yes, ma'am. The rails were already cut. I just had to bring them down and put them up."

"You must be feeling much better now."

"Thanks to you and Susanna," he said.

"Nonsense." But she looked pleased. Susanna looked positively delighted. He doubted that Susanna would be able to hide an emotion if she wanted to, and such a deception would certainly never occur to her on her own. She was completely open, which probably was one of the major reasons why he persisted in thinking of her as a child.

He had some of the eggs and wished they had some crisp fried trout to go with them. He had not had time to fish lately, and he missed it, both the pleasure of it and the resulting food. A diet of eggs and corn bread was filling but not exactly exciting.

"Oh, I almost forgot to ask you," Mrs. Guynon said.

"Yes, ma'am?"

"Susanna and I will be going to town tomorrow. Can we bring you anything?"

She knew there was some reason why he was not going to Ben Frake's store any longer, although he had never quite told her why. So the offer was more than just a neighborly gesture. If he would not be comfortable dealing there, she would handle the shopping for him. He appreciated it.

"We're out of coffee," he said. The "we" came out quite automatically, without forethought, although it certainly was not the sort of thing he had ever been accustomed to saying in the past. "And I could use some tobacco." He blushed. "But I couldn't ask you to buy that."

"Nonsense," she said again. "No one around here tends to my business, and I don't mix into theirs. I wouldn't feel at all awkward about purchasing tobacco for you. Lord knows I did it often enough for my late husband."

"Mama?"

"Yes, dear?"

"I know where there's some tobacco, Mama."

"You do?"

"In Daddy's big box."

"Big box?" Mrs. Guynon seemed puzzled for a moment. "In his trunk, you mean."

Susanna nodded.

Mrs. Guynon smiled. "I had almost forgotten about the things of Phil's. There may well be some tobacco there. You are certainly welcome to it, Mr. Smith, if it hasn't dried out by now. He kept his tobacco in a humidor, so it may be all right still."

"That's very kind of you, ma'am."

"I don't know why I never thought of this before, Mr. Smith, but there may be any number of Phil's things that you could use. He had some kind of a gun, too. I don't know anything about such things, but you might want to use that. If you wanted to hunt, I mean. Or—"

Smith shook his head. "No. Thank you, but . . . no."

"But there are any number of deer and—"

"No," he said again, just short of being rudely sharp with her. "Thank you, but I do not hunt."

She looked at him closely for a moment, seemed to be

assessing him. Then she nodded. "As you wish, Mr. Smith."

"Thank you."

He smiled at her, but the atmosphere in the room was very slightly strained throughout the rest of the meal. It was not until later, when he was reading to Susanna and Mrs. Guynon was putting the dishes away, that he began to relax again.

CHAPTER 38

"My nephew tells me that you wanted to see me, Mr. Smith. He said you may have had a change of heart about our proposals."

"Your nephew is a liar, Mr. Wheeler."

Smith looked beyond Wheeler's shoulder to where Tuck stood leaning insolently against the doorframe of Smith's house.

"Among his other poorer qualities," Smith added dryly.

The two had ridden into the yard, dismounted and come to the door uninvited. Smith had given in to courtesy and asked Wheeler in. He had not been so inclined with Tuck.

Wheeler looked confused. Then angry. "But—"

"I've had no change of opinion, Mr. Wheeler. I am not likely to. No matter how much pressure you apply. For reasons we have already discussed."

"Now see here," Wheeler sputtered. "I didn't come all this way to listen to insults, sir. I did not. I was told you wished to see me, Mr. Smith, and I was considerate enough of you to come, but by God, sir—"

"I already told you, Mr. Wheeler. Your nephew is a liar. I don't want him anywhere on my land again. Ever. Is that understood, Wheeler? He is not welcome here. As for the extent of your own knowledge and participation, sir—"

Wheeler was no longer listening. He had colored a dark red. He blustered and burbled, too upset at the moment to speak coherently.

Furious, he shook a fist under Smith's nose, then turned and stalked out toward the waiting horses.

Tuck remained where he was for a moment to give Smith a narrow-eyed look of hatred. Then he wheeled and followed his uncle outside.

This time Smith was able to contain his own anger. That pleased him. He felt better than he had in some time.

CHAPTER 39

Smith carried a chair down to the field and propped it against one of the newly reset posts so he could wait in comfort. He did not believe he would be spending the evening alone. He was right. He heard them approach sometime before midnight. The only thing that surprised him was that Tuck was not alone. He had not expected Asa Wheeler's nephew to let anyone else in on their clandestine activities.

Tuck already had his rope in his hand and was shaking a loop out, ready to drop it over a fencepost and do some pulling, when he saw Smith sitting there watching.

"What are you doing here?" Tuck asked. He sounded genuinely surprised.

"That's a damned strange question," Smith told him. "More like what I should be asking you. Except that I already know what you're doing here tonight."

The cowboy who was with Tuck edged his horse closer to Smith's chair and asked Tuck, "Is this the yellowbelly you told me about?"

Tuck nodded.

"I thought you said he'd be hiding in the house," the cowboy said.

Tuck shrugged.

The cowboy turned back to Smith and gave him a speculative look of appraisal. "You gonna fight us, man?" He did not sound particularly worried by that prospect. Just interested.

There was no way Smith could answer that question. He reached into a pocket and remained where he was.

"Ignore him," Tuck said. He kneed his horse closer to the fence and pulled his arm back, ready to flip his loop over a post.

Smith took one of the small stones he was carrying and threw it. He threw it no harder than he thought he had to. He did not want to hurt the horse.

The stone bounced off the shoulder of Tuck's horse, and the animal shied.

"Hey," the other rider shouted.

Smith tossed another rock. It hit the second horse in the forehead, and the sorrel bolted. It jumped forward, came up short against the fence and whirled, almost unseating its rider.

"Damn you," the cowboy bellowed.

Smith threw another stone, this time harder, striking the sorrel on the rump and sending it into a plunging run uphill away from the field.

Tuck jumped down from his skittish mount and dropped the reins. He charged forward, his punch starting long before he was within striking distance and whistling toward Smith's jaw. Smith ducked, pulling his head aside and sticking out one leg. Tuck tripped over Smith's ankle and went sprawling into the dirt.

"I don't want to hurt you," Smith said calmly, "but I don't want to see you destroy my fence again either. What do you think we ought to do about that?" He leaned forward and propped his elbows on his knees. He was still seated in the chair.

"Damn you." Tuck came to his feet with his fists balled and ready to fight. He looked past Smith in time to see his horse, still nervous and unsettled, race off to join the sorrel that had already run away.

"Damn it!" Tuck roared.

"Go home," Smith advised. "Even if you did haul the fence down again, I'd be here to keep the cattle out. And I'd only put it up again. Go home, Friar. Or I just may have to have a few words with some folks about the kinds of things you've been doing."

Tuck was angry, but he was also distracted. His horse had run off, and he was not at all sure that his partner would see it and be able to recover it. Having to walk back to camp would get him a horse laugh for sure. And he was the new foreman. The crew was not properly respectful of him anyway. If he had to walk back that would only get worse.

He looked from Smith to the darkness into which the horse had disappeared and back to Smith again.

"Go home," Smith said again softly.

"Later," Tuck hissed. "I ain't done with you by a long shot, mister."

"Leave me be," Smith said wearily. "You really and truly ought to leave me be, Tuck."

"You do what Asa wants, mister, and I will. But first you look him up an' ask him real nice could you please let him have what he wants with that little ditch. You do that, and I'll leave you be. But if you don't, or if you open your yap just the least little bit, and I'm gonna have you for lunch. And that's a promise."

Smith shook his head sadly. "Go home," he whispered.

Tuck leaned over to brush the dirt off his jeans, picked up the rope he had dropped when his horse shied and began walking in the direction the horse had run.

CHAPTER 40

Mrs. Guynon's glance shifted from her teacup to her hands, fingers knotted and twisting in her lap, and back to the cup again. She had not met his eyes with hers since she had first gotten here, but she had not yet been able to bring herself to raise whatever it was that had brought her. Most worrisome of all was the fact that she had not allowed Susanna to come inside. The girl was out in the barn feeding wisps of hay to Jack and Jake, one stem at a time.

"If for any reason," Smith said, trying to make it easier for her. He coughed into his fist. "If there is some reason that, uh, it would be awkward for you to, uh, be seen in my company again, well, I would understand, Mrs. Guynon."

That was a lie, really. He did not understand it at all. But he knew *some*thing had been told about him in the town. Otherwise Frake, the Byrneses, the Russells, none of that would have happened.

However little he knew about the cause, though, he could certainly understand and fully appreciate the weight of social pressures.

Smith sighed. He would miss Susanna. Mrs. Guynon too in a way. But it was really Susanna he would miss the most. He had become fonder of the girl than he had realized. Or intended.

"Truly I will understand, ma'am."

Mrs. Guynon's chin came up and she met his eyes. There was a spark of anger in her.

"I am neither a fool nor a coward, Mr. Smith."

He blinked. "Of course not."

"Then allow me the courtesy, please, of listening before you leap nobly ahead and cut your nose off to spite your face."

"Ma'am?"

"You are sitting there assuming, Mr. Smith, that I would believe the awful things they are saying about you." She sniffed. "This when I am one of the two people in the world, three, who would know absolutely that the whispers are false."

"But—"

"Mr. Smith, my difficulty is in how to approach this subject with some degree of . . . decency. If you know what I mean."

"I'm sorry, but I don't."

"Exactly what I thought, Mr. Smith. You don't even know what they are saying, do you, yet your stiff-necked pride won't allow you to ask. Isn't that it, Mr. Smith?"

This time it was his eye that wavered and left hers.

"I thought so." Mrs. Guynon sniffed again. "In all my years of marriage to Mr. Guynon, there were some certain subjects that were not discussed between us. It isn't easy for me to . . . make this explanation now, you see."

He said nothing. He did not see, of course, but apparently he was about to.

"What I must tell you, Mr. Smith, and I do *not* want Susanna to hear, is that in town there have been rumors that you took"—she looked down toward the cup of cooling and untasted tea—"that you have been taking . . . liberties . . . with my Susanna."

Smith was barely able to stifle a gasp of outrage.

"I learned of it yesterday evening, Mr. Smith. By way of sympathies expressed. Humph. Sympathies, my foot. Gossip was what they were after. The nasty biddies wanted to get all the horrid details. That is what they wanted. Believe you me, Mr. Smith, I gave them the details too."

She blushed. "Not . . . you know. Nothing about what happened that time." She looked at him again. "But I certainly gave them an earful about you and your relationship with Susanna, I can tell you that. Why, you've been the brightest spot in that child's life since her father passed on. And I told them so, although let me tell you that wasn't what they wanted to hear. Humph."

She was angry now, her eyes fairly snapping. "It wasn't what they wanted to hear, I can tell you, but they heard it anyway. And would you believe it, that Emily Russell had the gall to bring it up within Susanna's hearing? Let me tell you, I had to do some fancy shooing before she understood what was being suggested and blurted out the truth. She never has learned how to lie, you know, and I couldn't bear the idea of what might happen to her if anyone knows what happened with that animal cowboy. It could have happened anyway with this awful lie about you. The effect would have been the same since everyone believed that, well, that untrue things had taken place. Even though they didn't. The lie would have been just as bad as the truth. But I put rest to that lie, let me tell you."

"I didn't know," Smith said lamely. "If I had known that it could affect Susanna . . ." He spread his hands.

"Exactly," Mrs. Guynon said. She stood, still agitated. "Let me tell Susanna she can come in now. Then I'll start dinner."

Smith nodded. He was not really paying that much attention to her, though. There was a knot of dark anger churning in his stomach. This was twice now that John

Friar had harmed Susanna. It was only the child's innocence of nature that had kept her from being devastated the first time. But this lie could have been even worse, because it could have made her the victim of any number of lecherous, stupid youths. She had been almost unaffected by the one assault, but he did not know if she could have survived more.

Mrs. Guynon paused on her way to the door. "Mr. Smith."

"Ma'am?"

"It is one thing to turn the other cheek. That is in the Book. It would be quite another to allow wolves to prey on defenseless lambs. I believe you should think about that, Mr. Smith."

She went on to the door and called her daughter. The subject was not raised again, and she did not try to elaborate on her final comment.

CHAPTER 41

Smith brooded through most of the night. He had ample opportunity to think. As a precaution he took his chair down to the field again and sat there, catnapping, dozing, tottering very nearly off onto the ground, through most of the night.

When he finally concluded that John Friar and friends were not likely to come again that night he carried the chair back up to the house.

Tired as he was, though, instead of going straight to bed the way his gritty eyes and foggy brain demanded, he lighted his reading lamp, opened the trunk at the foot of his bed and rummaged in the bottom.

It took him a moment to find the item he wanted. While he searched he took some pains to avoid a bulky packet in the right rear corner wrapped in oilcloth.

Eventually he found what he wanted and pulled it out, an old, leather-bound black volume that had seen generations of use. The spine had been broken and the binding scuffed. The pages were smudged but the writing was still legible.

Sighing and reluctant, Smith left the trunk standing open and carried the book to his chair. He spread it open at random in his lap and tried to make sense of the beautiful but meaning-shrouded King James language.

The words on the pages swam and blurred. He had no

idea what he was looking for or whether he could recognize it if he did find it.

All he knew for sure right now was that his days of peace seemed to have ended, and he wished he could turn back the calendar.

He closed his eyes, intending to rest them only for a moment. When he opened them again it was past dawn, and he was overdue for his choring. He put the heavy volume back into the trunk and hurried out to the barn.

CHAPTER 42

He strode past the counters and shelves without a sideways glance, eyes front, back straight and head high. Frake was there, of course. So was Russell. Russell was fingering through a small selection of mill files. Smith looked the man in the eye and then Frake. To hell with the both of them, he told himself.

Frake was unable to meet his eyes, but Russell's reaction was one of belligerence. It was a common enough reaction to acute embarrassment, Smith knew.

Smith stopped in front of the bank of wooden pigeon-hole boxes that constituted the United States Post Office and waited silently for Frake to come and take his letters and postage. Frake hurried to him.

"Smith, I'm sorry as hell. The things I said . . . Mrs. Guynon explained, well, a great deal. The other day. We just didn't know . . . I mean we heard . . . well, you understand, I hope. And that business about your eggs. I didn't mean that, Smith. I want you to know that. I mean, you've been a good customer for years. You know? Never any problems with your accounts. And . . . well . . ."

"Three letters," Smith said coldly. "I believe that should be nine cents." He laid down a half dime and four pennies, put the letters beside them and shoved it all across the counter top toward Frake.

The storekeeper sighed and nodded. "Of course." He sighed again. "I'm sorry, Smith." He collected the coins and the letters, took stamps from a small drawer to put on the folded paper that had been fashioned into makeshift envelopes and dropped the letters into a small pouch without looking at the addresses.

He must have been curious, Smith realized, but Frake was being on his best behavior today.

It came as something of a shock for Smith to realize it himself, but this would be the first time Stillwater Smith had ever mailed anything since the post office was established. Once in a great while he had received a catalog through the mails, but any ordering he had done in recent years had always been through Frake.

Those days were over, Smith reflected bitterly. Still, it felt a little strange now to be sending mail out, even if it was just to possible buyers for pickled eggs.

It had been—he had to think far back for it—just after the war since Smith had had reason to send a letter to anyone. That long. Odd, it had not seemed so very long, but it was. The time had gone and he had scarcely noticed it in the isolated, insulated protection of home and pond and habit.

That long. Hard to believe.

Frake dropped the money into the cashbox, gave Smith an apologetic look and shook his head. It was obvious that he wanted to say more, but there was nothing left for him to say. After a moment he turned away.

Russell would have heard the same denials of the accusations that had been made about Smith, but his response was still one of covering his errors with more error. He bristled and rolled his shoulders as if loosening them for a fight.

The man could have turned his back. Instead he opened his mouth.

"Don't come at me with your holier-than-thou crap,

Smith. You might have that poor woman and her half-wit daughter fooled, but you're still a damned coward, man. Too yellow to raise a hand to defend yourself. That's a coward in my book, mister, and I haven't forgotten it."

Smith looked at him, lips drawn into a thin, wry smile. "I'm sure you haven't, Russell," he agreed. It occurred to him, but probably not to Russell, that Smith had said nothing that might be considered remotely holier-than-thou. Unless, of course, use of the mails had become a holy act while Smith was not looking.

"You're a damned coward," Russell repeated angrily.

Smith looked at him for a moment with something close to pity. Then laughed. He turned and walked back outside.

"Damn you," Russell yelled after him.

Smith was not paying any particular attention to the man, though.

That was something he had gotten rather good at over the years, Smith reflected as he gathered up his hitch weights and dropped them onto the floor of the driving box.

He had paid perhaps too little attention to a great many things since he settled into his quiet, comfortable rut of isolation. He had taught himself to ignore perhaps too much.

He was still thinking about what Mrs. Guynon had told him last evening.

CHAPTER 43

Smith left the book open in his lap and fingered the bridge of his nose for perhaps the fifth or sixth time in the past hour. The gesture did nothing to relieve the eyestrain, but it made him feel better anyway. He knew good and well that it was simply the fact of stopping reading for a moment and resting his eyes that helped, but he went through the ritual of rubbing regardless. He wondered if it was possible to order spectacles out of a catalog. Probably, but how would he know what model, grind, whatever they called it, to ask for? That was one of the disadvantages of catalog shopping. He would not be able to try them before he bought.

And at that he was going to have to come up with the money somehow. He hoped he could find that market for pickled eggs. It would make a difference.

He reached into his pocket and pulled out his pipe and tobacco pouch. He was not running low on tobacco quite yet, but he was already rationing himself in anticipation of it in the future. Mrs. Guynon's contribution from her dead husband's supply helped.

He tamped the pipe full and scraped a match aflame. As he raised the match toward the bowl of the pipe he heard a flurry of movement from outside, a growl and then a loud barking.

Smith blew the match out and listened more closely. It was unusual for Joe to bark. Most unusual.

Smith stood and walked toward the door, stopping on the way to take a lantern down off the wall and light it. The pipestem was forgotten between his teeth.

Joe barked again, from slightly farther away this time.

The unmistakable crack of a rifle shot sounded in the night.

The dog yelped, and the rifle fired again.

Smith ran out into the yard yelling, although he did not know at what or at whom.

The pipe fell from his mouth, but he did not notice it go.

He ran blindly, the lantern still in his hand.

CHAPTER 44

Smith set the shovel aside and squinted into the glare of the dawn sun. The mound at his feet was small. Certainly not large enough to indicate the overwhelming sense of loss and grief he felt. His eyes were sore. It bothered him that he had cried for a dog when there had been so many men he had not wept for.

He stood at the side of the pond where he had buried Joe and looked around the valley. It had been a good place. Its beauty was boundless. Even now he appreciated what he saw around him although he was able to take no joy from it.

Taking his time about it he picked up the shovel and made his way back to the house. He stopped behind the barn to gather up the things he had found there. A scrap of rag and a tin of coal oil. The articles had been dropped behind the barn, close to where he had found Joe.

The dog had stopped Friar.

Smith owed Joe for that.

Calmly, with no hurry whatsoever, Smith went about his morning routine of chores. He fed the horses, fed and watered the hens and the chicks—soon enough he would have to separate the cockerels for butchering and decide whether to keep any of the young hens for future layers, how many of the mature hens to cull and how many to keep; there would be time for that later or perhaps there would not; he did not have to think about it now—and went back into the barn to brush the horses and water them.

A pang of regret clamped inside his chest. He did not have to feed Joe this morning.

He took his time, concentrating on the chores of the moment.

He would think about the other necessary chores in their own good time.

He was in no hurry at all now.

CHAPTER 45

He pulled the wagon to a halt and took his time about rigging the hitch weights, adjusting the clips fussily on the snaffle rings of the driving bits. The cowboys nearby snickered but said nothing. Smith ignored them.

When he was ready he turned to them. There were two of them. He supposed they were ostensibly watching over the herd of several hundred cattle which were grazing on the hillside below, but if so they were not working very hard at it. They had built a fire, which was how he had found them, and had a tin can of water boiling on the edge of it. One of them had a mouth organ in his hands, but at the moment he was watching Smith instead of making music.

"Where is Friar?" Smith asked.

"Tuck?"

Smith nodded.

One of the cowboys shrugged. The other looked blank.

"Did he warn you not to tell me? Is he afraid?" Smith prodded.

One of the men laughed. "That'll be the day. We've heard about you, mister."

"Then where is he?"

"What do you want with him?" the other man asked. Both of the cowboys looked like they were having a fine time with this meeting.

"We have something to discuss," Smith said calmly.

"Something personal." He paused. "Or were you there last night too?"

"Where?" the cowboy asked. But he was grinning as he asked it. He knew what had happened. He had heard about it or had seen it. It seemed to have pleased him.

Smith walked up the slope toward them.

The cowboys stood. The nearer of them gave his companion a nervous, worried look but was reassured with a wink and a grin.

They both knew, Smith thought.

He felt the old, familiar tingle of anticipation tighten in the pit of his stomach. He knew his expression was controlled and stony, but he could hear the rush of blood in his ears and feel the flow of it at his temples. It was something he thought he had forgotten, but he had not. He recognized and approved of it now.

He had sworn it would never happen again, but he had been wrong.

"No need to bother ol' Tuck," the second cowboy said cheerfully. "We can take care of this."

"All right," Smith said agreeably.

He reached the first man. Both of them were grinning at him now. They moved toward him, separating slightly to take him from both sides, raising their fists in fighters' poses. Chuckling and having fun.

Hot blood pounded a drumbeat in Smith's temples, and his breathing began to quicken.

The nearer man started to say something. He did not have time to finish it.

Smith hunched his shoulders and lashed out at him, his fist catching the cowboy flush on the jaw just as the man's mouth opened.

There was a satisfying crack as bone shattered, and the man screamed in pain.

He started to fall, and Smith kicked him in the face, on the already broken jaw, before he hit the ground.

Coldly, deliberately, Smith turned to face the other man. He could finish with the first one later.

And he would.

He knew that.

All the years of determined resolution and control were forgotten now.

Now there was only the cold, empty fury.

Patiently he moved in on the second cowboy. Ready. Waiting. Intending to hurt him, knowing that he would.

The cowboy gave his partner a panicked look and then stared with disbelief into Smith's eyes. He turned to run, tripped and fell.

Smith picked him up.

The cowboy turned, squirming, trying to kick Smith and to get away.

Smith began to beat on him.

CHAPTER 46

"Smith!"

He went to the door and stood in the shadow, watching, in no hurry. He was calm, but he could feel the rise again of the deliberate fury he had sworn over and over again that he would not permit himself. He could feel it, and he did nothing to try to stop it.

Tuck was out there. On his horse but not so damned arrogant this time. He looked ashen and worried. He had seen the two men then, must have received the message Smith left with them.

Tuck was flanked by two riders. Probably they and the ones Smith had already seen this morning constituted Wheeler's entire crew in the valley. Tuck had his carbine laid over the pommel of his saddle. That was the gun he would have used to kill Joe. Smith could feel the tightness at his temples.

He turned and went to the trunk and knelt in front of it. It was there. Oiled and wrapped and protected for all the years. He picked it up, cold and heavy in his hand, and pulled aside the wrapping.

It was an old gun. Dark and beautiful. A cap-and-ball 1860 Colt Army. Everything nowadays was cartridge-loaded and modern. Tuck and his friends would probably find this relic laughable. But Smith knew what it could do.

Smith held it in his hand, the heft and balance as familiar as if he had last used it only yesterday.

He knelt in front of the trunk with the gun in his hand and felt himself begin to tremble. Sweat came to his forehead, and he closed his eyes tight shut.

"No," he whispered aloud. He took in a deep shuddering breath. *"No!"*

He opened his hand and let the revolver tumble into the bottom of the trunk.

Abruptly Smith came to his feet. He turned his back on the trunk and walked out into the glare of the sunlight to where Tuck and his men were waiting.

Tuck's horse curveted nervously. There was no dog to upset the animal today. It was taking its cue from its rider, Smith knew.

He walked straight to Tuck's side, paying no attention to the men who were with him.

Tuck swallowed and blinked. He picked up the carbine and worked the lever.

Smith reached for it, pulled it out of Tuck's hands. He glanced down at the weapon. He had never really looked closely at one of these modern weapons. It interested him, but he could take the time to examine it later. He threw it aside, hard, blued steel and walnut spinning high into the air.

"Smi—"

Smith took a firm grip on Tuck's sleeve and pulled him off the horse.

Tuck screamed, trying to shout a command to his men, but the two riders sat where they were, neither of them willing to risk the damage that they had already seen on their companions.

Tuck curled himself into a tight fetal ball and began to cry. He made no effort to defend himself. Smith was only very dimly aware of the sounds Tuck was making. He

could hear much more clearly the sounds of his own fists
and feet smashing into John Friar's unresisting frame.

Friar's men watched silently, neither of them willing to
look at the other. They did not step down from their sad-
dles until Stillwater Smith had gone back inside the house,
and then they did so hesitantly, flinching and looking up at
every hint of noise they heard.

CHAPTER 47

The bit of hand-carved wood jiggled in a brisk up-and-down flurry, sending a series of ripples radiating out through the water around it. Smith took the pipe out of his mouth and called out, "Watch him now, Susanna. Get ready."

The bobber disappeared under the surface of the pond. "Now!"

Susanna snatched back on the pole. There was a tug of resistance somewhere deep in the water and then the bobber, line and now-empty hook burst clear of the surface. The girl turned and gave Smith a look of intense disappointment.

"Too hard, honey. Remember what I showed you."

Susanna looked like she might cry. Smith smiled at her. His expression was gentle and comforting. "It's all right, honey. You'll get him the next time."

She smiled back at him. "I'll remember, Stillwater. I really will."

"I know you will, honey." He watched closely while Susanna rebaited her own hook—an accomplishment of the first order and one she was proud to demonstrate—then returned the pipestem to between his teeth and turned to look at her mother.

Mrs. Guynon was seated on a folded blanket beside Smith's favorite rock. She had a sewing basket, and one of Smith's shirts was spread out in her lap. There was a tear up the back that she had insisted on mending before he washed it, even though the shirt was filthy and blood-spattered. She had not asked how the stains had come to be there, and he had not volunteered anything.

The afternoon sun was slanting low. Soon they would have to pick up and move down to the house for supper. Smith was getting hungry. He had not taken time for breakfast this morning and had forgotten about lunch. Now he was feeling the lack.

Smith heard the clatter of shod hoofs on rock and stood. He recognized the handsome bay horse and its bulky, stiff-necked rider. Smith stood where he was, waiting for the man to reach them.

If Wheeler wanted more of the same . . .

Smith shook himself, forcing back the unwanted rise that was trying to well up again. He took three slow breaths and felt the sense of calm return. That pleased him. He had been worried about his ability for control. A dam once broken may not easily be repaired. And he would not have wanted to do anything precipitous with Susanna so near. He looked at her, but she was concentrating on the bobber that sat motionless on top of the water. The little scrap of wood seemed to fascinate her even when it was idle, and Mrs. Guynon said she truly thought that the fishing was helping Susanna's ability to concentrate on other things too.

Wheeler was alone and as far as Smith could see was not armed. He certainly would not have come here alone to engage in a fistfight. Not at his age and condition.

Smith nodded and removed the pipe from his mouth as Wheeler came to a halt and dismounted. "Wheeler."

"Smith." Wheeler nodded to Mrs. Guynon, then motioned with his chin for Smith to follow. The two men walked out of Mrs. Guynon's hearing, Wheeler's horse trailing behind them.

Wheeler seemed unsure how to begin.

"If you are thinking of making a final offer . . . ," Smith ventured.

"No," Wheeler said quickly.

"What then?" Smith sucked on the pipe, but it had gone out. He struck a match and relighted it.

Wheeler looked away, his eyes roving across the surrounding peaks and down into the long, placid valley. "I had five men working up here this morning. You've sent three of them down for doctoring. They may not be the same again, Smith."

Smith looked at him calmly and drew on his pipe. "I may not be either," he said softly.

"What kind of man are you, Smith?"

"The kind who wants to be left alone."

"I— My sister is going to give me hell, Smith. She won't understand why I don't press charges against you for what you did to her boy."

"Will you tell her what her boy did to me?"

Wheeler turned his eyes away. "No," he admitted. He looked at Smith. "I didn't know any of that. Not until late this morning. I want you to know that. It's important for me to know that you understand that."

Smith nodded. "All right."

"You don't believe me, do you?"

"I believe you."

"Thank you." Wheeler looked away again. He pulled a cigar from his pocket, bit the end off and accepted a light from Smith. "Thank you," he repeated. "I suppose I still owe you an apology for what my nephew and my men did, but under the circumstances . . ."

"I understand." It was more of an apology than Smith

would have expected. Nor would it have really mattered if there had been none at all.

Wheeler looked at him closely. "By Godfrey, I believe you do at that. Would you mind if I asked you a personal question, Smith?"

Smith shrugged.

"I haven't any right, but . . . you say you are a man who wants to be left alone. I can understand that, I think, after . . . Anyway, I think I know who you are. But would you mind satisfying my curiosity about who you were? I have no right to know. I'm not claiming any such right. But I would like to know."

Smith sighed and turned to look toward the peaks. Oddly, after all these years, it hardly seemed to matter.

Smith stiffened, and his eyes opened wider. He had been ashamed. All these years, and he had never really realized that. But he had been. He jammed the pipestem back between his teeth and frowned. He had been ashamed.

"Are you all right, Smith?"

He shuddered. "Sorry." For a moment there he had forgotten both Wheeler and his question. He turned to look at the former major.

"A long time ago," he said slowly, "did you ever hear of a quartermaster officer named Waters?"

"It rings a bell somewhere. Wait a minute." Wheeler snapped his fingers. "Of course. Can't imagine how I ever forgot. A captain, I believe he was. S. T. Waters. A Southerner serving with the Union. They called him . . ." Wheeler's voice trailed away and his eyes widened as he stared at Smith.

"They called him Still Waters," Smith said in his slow, soft voice.

"Jesus," Wheeler breathed. "Congress gave you that special medal, didn't they?"

Smith dismissed that with a grunt. "I didn't want that either," he said. "I didn't want to fight at all. That was why I went into the Quartermaster Corps. It was supposed to be quiet. But I couldn't stay out. I couldn't see the Union destroyed."

"I'm trying to remember. It was something about a raid on Grant's stores. Across the river from Vicksburg?"

Smith shuddered again, but it was almost a relief to be able to consciously think about it again.

"They said you were a very quiet man. From a good family. They said you went berserk that day."

"Their cavalry tore down the flag. And I . . . got mad." He winced. "I haven't really wanted to remember that time."

Lord God, I was ashamed, he thought.

"No one should do the things I did."

But how could I not have realized.

"At least my family never thought so."

Have I been so weak?

"I didn't go back. After."

Or just so afraid to remember.

"It's been better. Here. Until now. Now I don't know."

Smith turned his eyes away again, toward the peaks.

He felt better. Lighter. In spite of what had happened this morning.

And this time—he searched inside himself carefully— this time there were no regrets.

This time he had stopped short of killing. He was pleased about that. Proud of it. He had been able to exercise some control. A little. He smiled. Enough. *He did not have to fear the darkness inside himself. Never again.*

"I can't change what has already happened, Capt"— Wheeler paused, then smiled—"Mr. Smith. But I can assure you there will be no more trouble between us. I hope you will accept my word on that."

Wheeler extended his hand on it.

Smith looked at him for a moment. Then reached out to the man.

In spite of everything he felt like a vast weight had been taken from him. He smiled at Wheeler and shook the man's hand.

The smile turned into a grin, and he felt a sudden sense of urgency. He wanted to get back to the pond. To Susanna. To the child's mother. "If you would excuse me now, Mr. Wheeler?"

"Of course, Mr. Smith. I just wanted . . ." He shrugged.

"I know. Thank you."

Wheeler stuck the butt of the cigar into his mouth and mounted the tall Cleveland Bay with some difficulty while Smith held the horse's head.

"Goodbye, Mr. Smith."

"Goodbye, Mr. Wheeler."

Wheeler turned the horse and would have waved, but Smith had already turned away. He was hurrying back to the pondside where the quiet, not unattractive woman sat beside a rock with a sewing basket at her side and a soiled, torn shirt in her lap.

Ripples spread over the calm surface of the pond as the girl's bobber disappeared again.

Smith broke into a run toward her side, shouting encouragement and instruction as he ran.

There was a curiously glad, happy note in the sound of his voice, Wheeler thought. He reined his horse downvalley, wondering as he rode just what in *hell* he was going to tell his sister.

One thing he knew for sure. When he saw that useless

nephew of his he was going to have to tell him just how lucky he had been.

Wheeler turned in his saddle and looked back up the hill toward the pond, but Smith did not see. The lean gray man and the woman were busy congratulating a very excited girl.

Wheeler shook his head.

Lord!